MEET THE FRONTIER BAD MEN—
AND THOSE WHO DARED TO CHALLENGE THEM

—Men like Leo Carver, a man everyone in the town of Canyon Gap liked so much, they all planned to turn up for his hanging.

—Men like Marshal Lou Morgan, who tried to save his citizens from a gold-mine swindler, only to learn that his own code of honesty and loyalty made him the biggest sucker in town.

—Men like champion rodeo rider Marty Mahan, whom they called yellow because of his fear of the outlaw bronc Ghost Maker, until he showed them the true color of courage.

—Men like the Herring brothers, a murdering robber gang that had the misfortune to interrupt the Cactus Kid when he was picking flowers for his girl—and ended up as part of the bouquet.

Meet these characters and many more in
Louis L'Amour's
THE OUTLAWS OF MESQUITE

Bantam Books by Louis L'Amour
Ask your bookseller for the books you have missed.

NOVELS

BENDIGO SHAFTER
BORDEN CHANTRY
BRIONNE
THE BROKEN GUN
THE BURNING HILLS
THE CALIFORNIOS
CALLAGHEN
CATLOW
CHANCY
THE CHEROKEE TRAIL
COMSTOCK LODE
CONAGHER
CROSSFIRE TRAIL
DARK CANYON
DOWN THE LONG HILLS
THE EMPTY LAND
FAIR BLOWS THE WIND
FALLON
THE FERGUSON RIFLE
THE FIRST FAST DRAW
FLINT
GUNS OF THE TIMERLANDS
HANGING WOMAN CREEK
THE HAUNTED MESA
HELLER WITH A GUN
THE HIGH GRADERS
HIGH LONESOME
HONDO
HOW THE WEST WAS WON
THE IRON MARSHAL
THE KEY-LOCK MAN
KID RODELO
KILKENNY
KILLOE
KILRONE
KIOWA TRAIL
LAST OF THE BREED
LAST STAND AT PAPAGO
  WELLS
THE LONESOME GODS
THE MAN CALLED NOON
THE MAN FROM SKIBBEREEN
THE MAN FROM THE
  BROKEN HILLS
MATAGORDA
MILO TALON

THE MOUNTAIN VALLEY WAR
NORTH TO THE RAILS
OVER ON THE DRY SIDE
PASSIN' THROUGH
THE PROVING TRAIL
THE QUICK AND THE DEAD
RADIGAN
REILLY'S LUCK
THE RIDER OF LOST CREEK
RIVERS WEST
THE SHADOW RIDERS
SHALAKO
SHOWDOWN AT YELLOW
  BUTTE
SILVER CANYON
SITKA
SON OF A WANTED MAN
TAGGART
THE TALL STRANGER
TO TAME A LAND
TUCKER
UNDER THE SWEETWATER
  RIM
UTAH BLAINE
THE WALKING DRUM
WESTWARD THE TIDE
WHERE THE LONG GRASS
  BLOWS

SHORT STORY COLLECTIONS

BOWDRIE
BOWDRIE'S LAW
BUCKSKIN RUN
DUTCHMAN'S FLAT
THE HILLS OF HOMICIDE
LAW OF THE DESERT BORN
LONG RIDE HOME
LONIGAN
NIGHT OVER THE
  SOLOMONS
THE OUTLAWS OF MESQUITE
THE RIDER OF THE RUBY
  HILLS
RIDING FOR THE BRAND
THE STRONG SHALL LIVE
THE TRAIL TO CRAZY MAN

WAR PARTY
WEST FROM SINGAPORE
YONDERING

SACKETT TITLES

SACKETT'S LAND
TO THE FAR BLUE
  MOUNTAINS
THE WARRIOR'S PATH
JUBAL SACKETT
RIDE THE RIVER
THE DAYBREAKERS
SACKETT
LANDO
MOJAVE CROSSING
MUSTANG MAN
THE LONELY MEN
GALLOWAY
TREASURE MOUNTAIN
LONELY ON THE MOUNTAIN
RIDE THE DARK TRAIL
THE SACKETT BRAND
THE SKY-LINERS

THE HOPALONG CASSIDY NOVELS

THE RUSTLERS OF WEST
  FORK

NONFICTION

EDUCATION OF A
  WANDERING MAN
FRONTIER
THE SACKETT COMPANION:
  A Personal Guide to the
  Sackett Novels
A TRAIL OF MEMORIES:
  The Quotations of Louis
  L'Amour, compiled by
  Angelique L'Amour

POETRY

SMOKE FROM THIS ALTAR

THE OUTLAWS
OF MESQUITE

Frontier Stories by
Louis L'Amour

BANTAM BOOKS
NEW YORK • TORONTO • LONDON • SYDNEY • AUCKLAND

Editor's Note

The Author's Notes preceding each of the stories you are about to read are adapted from recording sessions conducted with Louis L'Amour for his Introductions to the audio dramatizations of his short stories, available from Bantam Audio Publishing on cassette tapes.

THE OUTLAWS OF MESQUITE

A Bantam Book
Bantam hardcover edition / June 1990
Bantam paperback edition / June 1991

ISBN 0-553-28714-1

Published simultaneously in the United States and Canada

Bantam Books are published by Bantam Books, a division of Bantam Doubleday Dell Publishing Group, Inc. Its trademark, consisting of the words "Bantam Books" and the portrayal of a rooster, is Registered in U.S. Patent and Trademark Office and in other countries. Marca Registrada. Bantam Books, 666 Fifth Avenue, New York, New York 10103.

PRINTED IN THE UNITED STATES OF AMERICA

OPM   0 9 8 7 6 5 4 3 2 1

Contents

The Outlaws
of Mesquite

Author's Note

The Mesquite I wrote about in this story is a rustler town, a holdup man's town, and it's quite unlike most towns in the West.

In more traditional towns, there were generally two sections. There was the part where the saloons and the red-light district were, what we still refer to today as the wrong side of the tracks, where most of the rough stuff like gunfights went on. On the other side there were churches and schools and citizens carrying on their lives the way normal people would.

Sometimes all the law-abiding people knew about the gunfights across the way was the sound of gunfire. They didn't know who was shooting whom until they heard about it later.

Milt Cogar was at the corral watching the paint when Thacker walked down from the store. "You'd better get out of this town, boy. They are fixin' to make trouble for you."

Milt turned around and looked at the big, clumsy man, his shirt stuffed into his trousers and held there by a rope belt. Thacker never seemed to have a full beard and always seemed to need a shave. His watery blue eyes looked vague. He rolled his quid in his jaws and spat.

"It's what I'm tellin' you, son. You done me a favor or two."

"Why should they be after me?" Cogar demanded. He was a lean young man with a dark, leatherlike face. His eyes were almost black, and keen.

"Spencer wants your horses. You know that. He sets a right of store by good horseflesh, and he's had a thorn in his side ever since you rode into the valley. Anyway, you're a stranger, and this country don't cotton to strangers."

Milt Cogar hitched his gun belts and stared at Thacker. "Thanks. I'll not forget it. But betwixt the two of us, this country has reason to be afraid of strangers."

Thacker's eyes shifted uneasily. "Don't you be sayin' that aloud. Not around here. And don't you tell nobody what I said."

Thacker drifted off down toward his shack, and Milt Cogar stood there, uncertainly. He was not ready to drift, nor did he like being pushed, but he had sensed the undercurrent of feeling against him.

Mesquite was a rustler town. It was a holdup man town, and he was a wild horse wrangler and a drifter. H threw the saddle on the paint and cinched it down. Al the while he was thinking of Jennie Lewis, for sh was the reason he had stayed on at Mesquite.

Milt Cogar was no trouble-hunting man. He knew tha of himself and he told that to himself once more. In nearl thirty years of drifting, he had kept clear of most of th trouble that came his way. Not that he hadn't had hi share, for times came when a man couldn't dodge fights This could be that kind of time.

Dan Spencer was ramrodding the town. He was th big wheel. Milt had seen the big man's eyes trailing hir down the dusty corner of road that did duty as Mesquite main street. There were only four buildings on that street and a dozen houses. Jennie lived in the house back unde the cottonwoods with Joe and Mom Peters.

Spencer wasn't only big and rough. He was slick. H was slicker than blue mud on a side hill, only he didn look it. Milt was a top hand at reading sign, and he coul read the tracks years left across a man's face. He knev what manner of a man Dan Spencer was, and what t expect from the others, from Record and Martinez.

It was a mean little place, this valley. The scattering o ugly, unpainted frame buildings, the hillsides covered witl scrub pine and juniper, the trail a dusty pathway throug the pine and huge, flat-faced boulders. There was waterhole, and it was that which had started the town And somewhere back in the cliff and brush country ther was a canyon where Spencer and his boys backed up thei stolen cattle.

Thacker was right. He should throw a leg over hi horse right now and light a shuck out of here. If he stayed there would be trouble, and he was no gunfighter lik Spencer or Record, nor a knife-in-the-belly killer lik Martinez. He should light out of here right now, but ther was Jennie Lewis.

Jennie was eighteen now, a slim, lovely girl with sof

gray eyes and ash-blond hair. She looked like the wind could blow her away but there was quick, bubbling laughter in her, and sometimes a look in her eyes that touched something away down inside of a man.

She was a casualty of the trail. Cholera had wiped out her family, and Joe Peters had found her, ten years old and frightened, and carried her home. Only now she was big enough and old enough for Spencer to see, and what Dan Spencer wanted, he took.

Nobody in town would stop Spencer. There were twenty-seven people in Mesquite, but those who weren't outlaws were shy, frightened people who made themselves obscure and came and went as silently as possible, fearful of speaking lest Dan Spencer lay eyes upon them.

That was how it had been until Milt Cogar rode into town with his catch of wild horses, sixteen head of them, and all fine stock, and most of them broke to ride. Milt was going on through, but he stopped by the waterhole with his horses, and while they drank he talked with Jennie.

"You've beautiful horses," she said wistfully. "I never saw anything so beautiful, not even the horses that Spencer has."

"They are nice." Cogar was a man unused to the sound of his voice, for he lived much alone. "That's one of the reasons why I catch them. I like working with horses."

She was standing near one of them, and the black put out a friendly nose, and she touched it. The horse did not shy.

"You would never guess they had ever been wild," she said wonderingly. "They are so gentle."

"Most horses are nice folks, ma'am," he said. "They like people. You teach one he doesn't have to be afraid, and right away he gets mighty curious and friendly. For the first few days you just keep them around, no sudden movements, no violence. Just keep a firm hand on them, and feed them well.

"Horses when frightened can't think, not even so much as people, but once they know a man, they'll trust him to take them anywhere at all."

She looked at him thoughtfully. "You must be a kind man," she said gently. "Most men around here break their horses rough."

He flushed and looked away, feeling the slow red on his face and neck and hating himself for being self-conscious. "I don't know about that, ma'am."

Hurriedly, he tried to change the subject. "Your folks live here?"

A shadow touched her face. "No, they are dead, long ago. I live with Joe Peters over on the sidehill. He and Mom took me in when I was a child." Her eyes went to his. "You aren't staying here?"

"I was figuring on drifting through," he said, "down toward the canyon country. I got me a little place down there, and I figured to rest up for a while."

"It must be nice to go wherever you want," she said slowly, shifting the heavy wooden bucket in her hands. "This is an awful place!"

The sudden feeling in her voice shocked him. "Why don't you leave?"

"I can't. Dan Spencer wouldn't let me, not even if I found a way to get out."

"Spencer? What's he to you?" Milt Cogar pushed his black hat back on his head and looked at her, seeing the softness in her eyes, and the worry, too. Yet it was more than worry: it was fear.

"He runs Mesquite and everybody in it. He . . . wants me."

"Do you want him? You aim to marry him?"

She flushed anew. "I've not much to say about it here. If he wants me, there's nobody to stop him. As for the rest of it, he hasn't said anything about marrying."

Milt Cogar felt chill anger rising within him. "Who does this Spencer think he is?" he demanded. "Nobody can take a girl unless she wants to go! This country's free!"

"Not in Mesquite, it isn't! This is Dan Spencer's town, and nothing happens in it he don't like. You'd better keep him from seeing your horses, too. He'll want them."

"He'll trip himself up gettin' them!" Cogar said decisively. His eyes went to Jennie's face. "Ma'am, why don't you mount up and ride out of here? If you want to go, I'll see you get safe to the Ferry. Once across the river, you can head down toward Prescott or somewhere you'd be safe."

"Oh, if I only could—" Her voice died, and Milt looked up.

A burly, heavy-shouldered man with two guns was standing across the waterhole.

"If you could what?" the burly man asked. Then his eyes shifted to Milt, and from him to his horses, which he studied with a slow, appraising look, then back to Cogar. "Who are you?"

Milt looked at him with careful eyes. There was danger in this man, but he had faced danger before.

"I'm a man ridin' through," Milt said. "Who are you?"

Spencer stiffened. "Dan Spencer's the name, and I run this town."

Milt lifted his eyes insultingly toward the collection of miserable shacks. "Must keep you busy," he said.

"Not too busy but what I could teach you some manners!" Spencer's voice rang harshly. He walked around the waterhole, hands swinging at his sides. "Jennie, you go on home!"

Only an instant did the girl hesitate, apprehension for Cogar in her eyes. Then she began backing away.

Spencer stopped, a dozen feet from Milt, and dropped his hand to his gun butt—then the hand froze where it was, and Dan Spencer's eyes bulged. He was looking into the muzzle of a .44 Winchester carbine. "Unbuckle your belt, and be careful!" Milt warned.

Dan Spencer's face was gray. Very slowly he moved his fingers to the belt and unbuckled it, letting the Colts fall. "Now take a step toward me," Cogar commanded.

The big man complied. Color was coming back into his face and with it the realization that Milt Cogar had shown him up in front of the girl. Yet there was little he could do. His guns were on the ground behind him now.

"Now, let me tell you something, Spencer." Cogar spoke quietly, but coldly. "You let me alone. I'm passing through Mesquite. I may decide to stay over a couple of days, but don't let that give you any ideas, because if you get tough with me, I'll kill you! Now pull your freight."

When Spencer was gone, Milt stooped and shucked the shells from Spencer's guns, then from the belt, shoving the shells into his pocket—all but a few. He stood there by his horses and, taking out his knife, worked for a few minutes over those shells. Then he fed them back into the guns. When he was about to mount and ride on, he heard a low call from the brush. It was Jennie.

He mounted and rode over to where she waited, leaving his horses tied in groups of four.

"You'd better go quickly!" she warned. "He'll kill you! It isn't only him alone. He has other men. Two of them are John Record and Pablo Martinez. Both are killers and with him nearly all the time."

Cogar looked down at the girl. He was a tall, spare man with a quiet, desert man's face.

"This is no place for a girl. You want to leave?" he said.

Hope flashed into her eyes. "Oh, I'd love to! But I've nowhere to go, and even if I wanted to, Spencer wouldn't allow it. Mom has wanted Joe to smuggle me away, but he's afraid."

"Well, you get back to your house and get together whatever you want to take along, but not much of it. You fix us a mite of grub, too. Then you slip out of the house, come daybreak, and meet me by that white boulder I can see just below town. I'll take you out of here, and see you get safe to help. You ain't afraid of me?"

Jennie looked at him quickly. "No, I guess not. You look like an honest man. Also I'm remembering you treat your horses kind. I trust you. Anyway," she added, "there's nobody else."

He grinned. "That makes it simple. You be there, now. We may have to ride fast."

When Milt Cogar had his horses bedded down on the edge of Mesquite, he studied the place warily. There was a saloon, a general store, a blacksmith shop, and an eating house. Leaving his carbine concealed near a clump of mesquite, he hitched his guns to an easier position and headed up the street. A heavy-bodied man with a stubble of beard showed on the saloon stoop. Milt avoided the place, rightly guessing it would be Spencer's hangout, and walked to the restaurant and went in.

A fat man with freckles and a fringe of sandy hair around a bald spot was cooking over an iron range. He glanced up.

"Fix me some grub," Milt suggested. "I'm sure hungry."

Red nodded briefly and, grabbing a big plate, ladled out a thick chunk of beef, a couple of scoops of beans, and some potatoes. Then he poured a cup of coffee from a battered coffeepot and picked up some sourdough bread.

Cogar ate in silence for a while, then glanced up. "You one of Dan Spencer's outfit?"

Red stiffened. "I run my own shebang. If Spencer wants to eat, I feed him. That's all I have to do with him."

"I heard this was his town."

"It is. All but me." The door pushed open as he spoke, and Thacker came in. He sat down heavily on a chair across the table from Milt Cogar.

"Nice horses you got," he said tentatively.

Milt glanced up, taking in Thacker with a glance. "They'll do," he agreed.

"Don't need a hand, do you? Sixteen horses are a bunch for one man."

"My horses are gentle. I can handle them."

Thacker's face flushed a slow red, and he glanced toward the sandy-haired cook. He said softly:

"I could use a mite of work now. I'm sort of short."

Milt Cogar could sense the big man's embarrassment and it stirred his quick generosity. "Might lend you a bit," he suggested, keeping his own voice low. "Would ten dollars help?"

Thacker's face glowed red, but there was surprise and gratitude in his eyes. "I ain't no hand to borry," he said, "and you ridin' through like you are." He spoke hesitantly. "I reckon I hadn't better."

Cogar pushed a gold piece across the table. "Take it, man, and welcome. I've been staked a couple of times with no chance to pay back, so forget about paying me. When you have it, stake some other hombre."

When Thacker had gone, Red turned around. "Heard that," he said, then jerked his head toward the way Thacker had gone. "He ain't much good, either, but he's got him a boy he fair worships. He'll buy grub for that kid with the money, you can bank on it."

It was later, by the corral, that Thacker had come to Cogar with his warning. It was unnecessary, for Milt knew what he was facing. He also knew he was going to ride out of that town with Jennie Lewis or there would be blood on the streets. Yet he was no fighting man unless pushed. He wanted to get her away without trouble, yet when he faced the facts, he knew that Spencer grated on his nerves, that the thought of the man ruling the helpless people of the town angered him.

Carefully, he looked over his horses, checking to see if any had injured feet, and stopping to talk and pet each one of them. They were fine stock, and would sell well, yet he never gentled a bunch like this without hating to part with them.

Up the street he could see lights going on in the saloon. He felt better with the meal under his belt, and he inspected his gun again. Spencer, Record, and Martinez, and half the town at least in cahoots with them. Nor could he expect any help. It was his game.

Milt backed up against a corral post and faced the town. He could watch from here. The horses liked to see him close. He dozed a little, knowing trouble would come later, if at all. For a while they would wait for him at the saloon, and that was a place he had no intention of going.

Darkness crawled over the hills and pushed patrols of shadow between the buildings and along the edge of the woods. More lights came on. Behind him a horse stamped and blew, and somewhere out on the desert, a blue quail called softly, inquiringly.

It was very quiet. A tin bucket rattled somewhere, and he could smell the oil on his guns. Once he got up and walked among his horses, talking softly to them. His eyes shifted toward the light in the cabin where Jennie lived.

It seemed strange, having a woman to think about. He was a lonely man, and like so many lonely men he knew how to value love, attention, and the nearness of someone. He remembered the dusty spun gold of her hair, and the slim figure under the faded dress. There was something fine about her, something that spoke of another world than the world of Mesquite, Dan Spencer, and his followers.

He grinned ruefully. After all, she was not his to think about. He had only offered to help her, and once she was safely away—well, who was he to expect interest from such a girl as that?

A door opened and closed, and he glanced toward the saloon, making out a dark figure on the porch. The pale blotch above it was the man's face, looking toward him. Yet the watcher could not see Milt, for the blackness of his body would merge with the blackness of the corral corner.

They were beginning to wonder if he was coming, and when. He sat perfectly still, keeping his ears ready for the slightest sound. He did not look directly at the figure, but near it, and he did not allow his gaze to become fixed. He must be wary and ready always.

Had it not been for the weariness of his horses he might have started with Jennie at night, but the horses needed rest, and tomorrow would be a hard, long day. Doubly hard if Spencer elected to pursue.

The man on the porch returned inside, and Milt Cogar arose and moved around to get the stiffness from his muscles. Suddenly, an idea came to him, and he turned toward the corral, staring within. His own horses were outside, but inside were a half-dozen cow ponies used by Spencer and others. For an instant, Cogar considered, and then he got busy.

A sorrel with a white face had stayed close to the corral bars and several times he had patted it a little. Now he went inside and, catching the halter, led it out and tied it near his own horses. By soft talk and easy movements, he succeeded in getting two more outside where he tied them in plain view of the saloon. Then he took the first four of his own horses and, walking them carefully, led them away down the trail.

When he was out of sight of the town, he tied them and returned. In four trips he had led all of his own horses to the same place. Then he untied the first four, knowing they would stay together. After that he walked back and saddled his gray gelding. The paint he had caught earlier was already saddled and waiting. He had bought the extra saddle from a busted cowhand down Las Vegas way, but now it was to come in handy.

He retrieved his rifle and slid it into the scabbard. Then he sat down and lit a cigarette. Twice in the next hour or so a man came to the saloon door and looked out. Each time he let the cigarette glow brightly.

From where he sat he could see the corner of the water trough in the corral, and a glow caught his eye. For a few minutes he studied it curiously, and then recognized it. The glow was that greenish, phosphorescent light from damp, rotten wood, such as he had often seen in swampy country, or after a period of heavy rains. Many times he had seen branches like that, greenish, ghostly fingers reaching into the darkness.

It gave him another idea and he got to his feet again and walked off a short distance. It was still visible. This would be just the added touch he would need to make his escape effective. He broke off a small bit of the wood and fastened it into the corral post where he had been sitting, and then moved out into the street. The glow was still visible, not so bright as a cigarette, but enough to fool anyone taking a casual glance toward the corral. They were, he was sure, waiting for him to fall asleep.

Once the phosphorescent wood was in place, he moved swiftly. Getting into the saddle, he led the gray horse behind him and moved across the valley toward the Peters cabin, where Jennie Lewis lived. Dismounting then, he concealed his horses in the timber, and moved up to the house. A quick glance through the windows, and he saw no one but Jennie, carrying dishes away from the table, and the two older people.

Stepping up to the back door, he tapped gently. There was a moment of silence within, then a question. "Who is it?" At his reply, the door opened and he stepped inside.

"We've got to go now," he said quickly. "My horses aren't ready for it, but Spencer's bunch are watching me, and we've got a chance to get away that may give us an hour or so of start."

Joe Peters was staring at him, his face pale. "Hope you make it!" he said. "I hate to think what Spencer will do when we don't tell him you're gone! He's apt to kill us both, or whup us!"

"We'll fix that," Cogar replied. "We'll tie you both. You can say I threw a gun on you."

"Sure!" Peters said. "Sure thing!" He turned to his wife, "Mom, you let me tie you, and then this hombre can tie me."

Jennie had not hesitated. When he spoke she had turned and gone into her room, and now she came out. Startled, he saw she had a pistol belt around her hips.

"Pa's gun," she said, at his question. "It might come in handy!"

They rode swiftly until they reached the edge of the settlement, and then swung around toward where Milt Cogar had left his horses. As they drew alongside, Milt got down to unfasten the ropes that tied them in groups of four. They might have to run, and he wanted nothing to tangle them up.

Suddenly, a dark figure moved from the shadow of the mesquite, and a low voice spoke softly. "I've got you covered. If you move I'll shoot!"

It was not Dan Spencer. But Record, perhaps?

"Who's moving?" he said calmly. "You're doin' a fool thing, buttin' in on this deal."

"Am I?" The man stepped out from the darkness of the mesquite, and Cogar could see his face. The man was slim, wiry and hard-jawed. The gun he held brooked no argument. "Anyway, I'm in. Dan Spencer will be pleased to find I've stopped you from gettin' away with his girl."

Milt Cogar held himself very still. There was only one way he could come out of this alive, and it required a gamble with his life at stake. The moment would come. In the meanwhile, he tried the other way, for which he had no hope.

"Folks won't let you steal this girl," he said. "They'll stand for everything but that."

"They'll stand for that, too," the man said. "Now turn around!"

"Stay where you are!" Jennie's voice was low, penetrating. "Johnny Record, I've got you covered. Drop that gun or I'll kill you!"

Record stiffened, but before he could realize that as long as Cogar was covered there was a stalemate, the girl's voice snapped again.

"You drop that gun before I count three or I'll shoot. One! Two! Thr—"

Her count ended as Record let go of his gun. Milt stepped up and retrieved it. Swiftly then, he spun Record around and tied him tightly, hand and foot.

In the saddle and moving away, he glanced through

e darkness toward Jennie. "I reckon as a hero I don't
unt for much, you gettin' us out of that fix!"

"What else could I do? Anyway, I'd never have had
e courage unless you were taking me away like this.
'ith a man to help, I'm brave enough, I guess."

They rode on, holding a steady if not fast pace. There
as small chance of them losing any pursuit. That would
ve to be met when it came. He couldn't leave his horses
hind, for they were all he had. He might need the
oney from their sale to help Jennie. She would be friend-
ss and alone.

The desert was wide and white in the moonlight, with
ly the dark, beckoning fingers of the giant cactuses or
e darker blotches of the mesquite or distant mountains.
e turned off the trail he had been following, heading into
e canyon country. This would be rough going, but there
ere places ahead where one might stand off an army.

Foothills crept out into the desert toward them, and
ey started the horses into a deep draw between two
rted arms of hills. The rock walls grew higher and
gher, and they lost the light, having only a small rectan-
e of starlit sky overhead. Milt took no time to rest, but
shed the horses relentlessly, taking no time for anything
t getting on.

He knew where he was going, and he knew he must
ake it by daylight. Jennie said nothing, but he could
nse her weariness, judging it to an extent by his own,
r her strength would not be equal to his.

Finally, the canyon opened out into a wide flat valley
the mountains, and he moved the horses into the tall
ass, giving them no rest, but pushing them diagonally
ross it. They were mounting toward the far wall of the
lley before he drew up.

"We'll stop here, Jennie," he said, "but we daren't
ve a fire."

He divided the blankets and rolled up in his. In a

moment, he was sound asleep. He was unworried abo
the horses, for they would be too tired to go far.

The sun on his face awakened him, and he came to
sitting position with a start. Jennie was sitting about
dozen feet away with his rifle across her knees.

Milt stared at her, red-faced. "I slept like a tende
foot!" he said, abashed.

"I'm not used to sleeping out, so I awakened earl
that's all. There was no need you being awake. Anywa
they just came into the valley."

"Spencer?"

"Three of them. They came out of the ravine ov
there and are scouting for our trail. They haven't found
yet."

"Probably not. There's wild horses in this valley a
their herd tracks are everywhere." Jennie looked tired b
her eyes were bright. "We'll saddle up and get going."

When they were moving again, he hugged the wall
the canyon, knowing they would scarcely be visible agai
its darkness. They pushed on steadily, and from time
time his eyes strayed to the girl. She rode easily in t
saddle, her willowy body yielding to every movement
the horse.

He found he liked having her there. He had nev
realized how nice it was to know there was someo
beside you, someone who mattered. That was the troub
It was going to be lonesome when she was gone. To avc
that thought, he turned in his saddle and glanced bac
They were coming, all three of them, and he had no mc
than a mile or two of leeway before they would catch u

Milt's mind was quick, and he knew this valley. T
hollow up ahead was the only possible chance. He rode
and turned the horses into it, backing them into the tre
along the hillside out of range. Jennie had followed I
glance when he looked back, and her face was pale.

When the horses were safely under the trees, he walk
back to the crest of the rise. It was a poor place 1
defense, yet nothing else offered. In the bottom of t

hollow one was safely out of range unless they circled around and got on the mountain behind it. If that happened, there would be small chance for either of them. Still, Milt thought as he nestled down into the grass, there were only three outlaws.

They came on, riding swiftly, and he knew they had seen the two of them ride into the hollow. Jennie moved up beside him.

"I can load your rifle," she whispered, "while you stand them off with the six-guns."

He nodded to indicate he understood, and lifted the .44 Winchester. When they were within rifle range, he sighted at them, then took the gun from his shoulder and let them come closer. At last he lifted the rifle again and put a shot into the ground ahead of them. They drew up.

"That won't get you no place!" Spencer roared. "You turn that girl loose and we'll let you go!"

Cogar made no reply, merely waiting. There was some talk down below, and then he called out. "You've come far enough. Don't advance any further!"

One of them, probably Martinez, although Milt could not be sure, wheeled his horse and started for the hollow at a dead run. Milt lifted the rifle and fired.

The rifle leaped in his hand, and Martinez yelled and threw up his hands. He went off the horse as it veered sharply and cut away across the grass. Martinez staggered to his feet and, one arm hanging limp, started back toward the other two outlaws.

Cogar let him go. He was not a killer, and wanted only to be let alone.

Four more horsemen were coming up, and were scarcely more than a half mile away. They came on, and drew up with Spencer, where they began to talk.

"That makes six of them out there, not counting Martinez," Cogar said. "Looks like we're in for it."

"You could let them have me," Jennie suggested. Her cheek was pillowed on her forearm, and her wide eyes on his face.

He did not take his eyes from them. "Don't talk fool-ishness! I said I'd take you away, and I will. My promises are good."

"Is your promise the only reason?"

"Maybe it is and maybe it ain't. Womenfolks always have to see things personal-like. If you can be got out of this alive, I'll get you out."

"You know, you're really quite good-looking."

"Huh?" He looked around, startled at the incongruous remark. Then as it hit him, he flushed.

"Oh, forget it! Looks ain't gettin' us out of this hole! What I'm afraid of is they'll get somebody on the moun-tain behind us, or else they'll fire the grass."

"Fire the grass?" Her head jerked up and her face went white. "Oh, no! They wouldn't burn us!"

"That outfit? They'd do anything if they got good and riled."

Some sort of a plan seemed to have been arrived at. Dan Spencer shouted again:

"One more chance! Come out with your hands up and we'll turn you loose! Otherwise we're comin' after you!"

They were barely within rifle range, and Milt Cogar knew the chips were down. His reply was a rifle shot that clipped a white hat from the head of a newcomer. They all hit dirt then.

"I wanted to get him then," Milt muttered. "That wasn't to scare him."

Milt was scared, he admitted to himself. He was as scared as he'd ever been, yet in another way, he wasn't. There was no way out that he could see, and if they fired the grass the only chance was a run for the horses and a wild break in an attempt to outrun the attackers. But there was small chance of that working, for there were too many of them. An idea came suddenly.

"You slip back there," he said. "Get the horses down into the hollow. We may have to make a break for it."

She glanced at him quickly, and then without a word, slid back down the slope and got to her feet. He heard a rifle spang, but what happened to the bullet, he didn't know, and then there was a volley and he knew what happened to all the rest. Two whipped by right over his head, and one of them burned him across the shoulders. He rolled over and crept to another position. He could see nothing to shoot at, yet a moment later there was a movement down below, and he fired twice, fast as he could ever the rifle.

The movement stopped, and he rolled over again, getting himself to a new position. If they got to the edge of the hollow, he was done for, but he couldn't watch all the terrain. A bullet nipped the grass over his head and he fired at the sound.

Stealing a quick glance backward, he saw Jennie coming out of the trees into the hollow with the horses. They seemed disturbed by the firing, and halted not far away.

Spencer yelled then, and instantly, without replying, Milt snapped a shot at the spot, then one left and one right of it. He heard a startled yelp, but doubted from the sound that his shot had more than burned the renegade.

"Get to your horse but keep your head down!" he warned Jennie. "Now listen: we're going out of here, you and I, and fast when we go. We're going to start our horses right down there into the middle of them, and try to crash through. It's a wild chance, but from the way they act, they are scattering out to get all around us. If they do, we won't have much chance. If we run for it now, right at them, they may get us, but we'll have a chance of stampeding their horses."

He swung into the saddle and they turned the herd of fifteen horses toward the enemy, then with whoops and yells, started them on a dead run for Spencer. The rim of the hollow and the tall grass gave them a few precious moments of invisibility, so when the horses went over the rise they were at a dead run.

Milt Cogar, a six-gun in each hand, blazed away over the heads of the horses at the positions of the attackers. He saw instantly that he had been right, for men were

already moving on foot off to left and right to surround the
hollow.

With a thunder of racing hoofs, the horses charged
down on Spencer's position, nostrils flaring, manes flowing
in the wind of their furious charge.

Milt saw Dan Spencer leap to his feet and throw up a
gun, but his shot went wild, and the next instant he
turned and fled. Johnny Record had started to move off to
the right, but he turned when he saw the charging horses
and threw his rifle to his shoulder. Cogar snapped a shot
at him, and the yells of the men ahead swerved the
horses.

There was a moment of startled horror as Record saw
death charging upon him, and then he dropped his rifle
and started to run. He never made it, and Milt heard his
death scream as he went down under the lashing hoofs.
And then the herd was racing away down the valley.

"Milt!" Jennie's cry was agonized.

He swung his horse and looked back. The gray had
fallen with her, spilling her over on the ground even as
she screamed. And running toward her was Dan Spencer.

Milt Cogar's horse was beside her in three bounds and
he dropped from the saddle, drawing as he hit ground.
His first shot was too quick, and he missed. Spencer
skidded to a halt, his face triumphant.

"Now we'll see!" he shouted.

The veins swelled in his forehead, and his eyes were
pinpoints of steel. His gun bucked in his hand, and Milt's
leg went out from under him, but even as his knee hit
ground, he fired. His bullet caught Spencer in the dia-
phragm, and knocked him back on his heels. Both men
fired again, but Dan Spencer's shot bit into the earth just
in front of Cogar, and he thumbed his gun, aiming low
down at the outlaw's body. Spencer backed up, his jaw
working, his eyes fiercely alive. Then a bloody froth came
to his lips, and Milt, cold and still inside, fired once more.
The outlaw's knees gave way and he pitched over on his
face.

Milt stared at the fallen man, fumbling at his belt for more cartridges. His fingers seemed very clumsy, but he finally filled the empty chambers. Jennie was hobbling toward him.

"I've sprained my ankle," she said, "but it's nothing!"

She dropped beside him, and gasped when she saw the blood on his trouser leg. "You're hurt!" she exclaimed.

"Not much," he told her. "Who's that coming?"

Her head came up sharply. Then her face whitened with relief. "It's Joe Peters! And Thacker!"

The two men walked up, the slender Peters looking even smaller beside the rope-girthed bulk of Thacker. Both men had rifles.

"You two all right?" Thacker demanded. The hesitation and fear seemed to have left him. "We hurried after you to help, but we got here late."

"What happened to the other men with Spencer?" Cogar asked.

"The horses got both Martinez and Record. We found one other man dead, one wounded. We kilt one our ownselves, and caught up the rest."

Red came up. "Reckon you started somethin', mister," he said to Milt. "When you took Jennie away so's Spencer couldn't have her, we decided it was right mean of us to let a stranger protect our women. So Thacker here, he seen Joe Peters, and a few others. Then we got together at my eatin' place and started cleanin' the town. We done a good job!"

Thacker grinned, well pleased with himself. "You two can come back if you want," he suggested. "This here deserves a celebration."

"Why, I'd like to come back, sometime," Milt said, "but right now I've got to get my horses down to my own ranch and into the pasture there. I'd take Jennie to see the place, if she'll go."

"A ranch might be nice," Jennie said. Her eyes smiled at him, but there was something grave and serious in their depths. "I might like it."

"Only if you come, I might want to keep you," Milt said. "It isn't going to be the same after this."

"Why should it?" Jennie said.

The gray had gotten to his feet and was shaking himself. Milt walked over to him, and his hand trembled as he examined the gelding's legs. When he straightened up, Jennie was facing him, and her lips looked soft and inviting.

"I reckon," Thacker said, pleased, "that we'll have to celebrate without them!"

Love and
the Cactus Kid

Author's Note

Nowadays when we see women riding in the West they're usually wearing blue jeans, but this was not the case during the time these stories take place. Up until World War I, or shortly thereafter, a woman wouldn't have been caught dead wearing pants anywhere. She wore a dress wherever she went.

Women never rode a horse astride unless they were miles from where anybody was likely to see them. Then they might. They rode sidesaddle, and sidesaddle only, with the dress very carefully draped over the side of the horse. I had an aunt, a very beautiful young woman, who rode that way, and she was something to watch.

In public a woman was very careful not to show any more than her ankles. And about the only time you got to see them was when she was getting out of a stage or down off a railroad train.

Chapter 1
Flowers for Jenny

Jenny Simms, who was pocket-sized and lovely, lifted her determined chin. "If you loved me, you would! You know you would! It's just that you don't love me enough! Why, just look at what the knights used to do for their ladies! And you won't even get me some flowers!"

"Flowers?" The Cactus Kid stared at her gloomily. "Now it's flowers! Girls sure do beat me! Where in this country would a man find flowers?"

His wave at the surrounding country where their picnic lunch was spread was expressive and definite. "Look at it! Ain't been a drop of rainfall in four months, and you know it! Scarcely a blade of grass that's even part green! Worst drought in years, and you want flowers!"

"If you loved me you'd get them!" Her voice was positive and brooked no argument. "If a man really loves a girl he can do anything!"

Her blue eyes flashed at him, and their beauty shook him anew. "Nesselrode, if you love me . . . !"

"Sssh!" he pleaded, glancing panic-stricken around. "If anybody heard that name they'd hooraw me out of the country. Call me Clay, or Kid, or anything but Nesselrode!"

"It's your name, isn't it? Nesselrode Clay. I see noth-

29

ing wrong with it, nothing at all! Furthermore"—she was
not to be diverted—"if you love me you'll get me some
flowers! I told the girls you were giving me flowers and
they laughed at me! They did. They said there were no
flowers closer than California, this time of year."

The Cactus Kid rolled a smoke and stared at it with
dark disgust. Women! He snorted. What they could think
of! Jenny could think of things nobody else would dream
of. That came of reading so many books, all romances and
the like. Made her look for a man on a white charger who
would do great feats to win her love.

Not that he wouldn't. Why right now, instead of being
on a picnic with Jenny, he ought to be out with the posse
chasing the Herring boys. There were three of them, and
all were gun-slick and tough. They had stopped the U.P.
train on a grade about fifteen miles from here, killed the
express messenger and the fireman. They had looted the
safe of forty thousand dollars in gold and bills. There was a
reward on them, a thousand apiece for Benny and Joe,
and four thousand for Red.

With the money he could buy some cows and stock
that little ranch he was planning on. He could set up a
home for a girl like Jenny to be proud of, and with his
know-how about cows they could soon be well off. But no,
instead of hunting for the Herrings, she wanted him to go
hunt flowers!

"It's little enough to do for me," she persisted. "All
you think of is running around shooting people in the
stomach! You ought to be ashamed, Nesselrode!"

He winced and started to speak, but his voice was lost
in the storm of words.

"If you don't bring me some flowers for my birthday,
Nesselrode, I'll never speak to you again! Never!"

"Aw, honey!" he protested. "Don't be like that! The
sheriff asked me particular to go along and hunt for the
Herrings. The boys'll think I'm scared!"

"Nesselrode Clay! You listen to me! If you don't get
me those flowers, I never want to see you again! And don't

you be shooting anybody, either! Every time you go to do something for me you get into trouble, shooting somebody in the stomach!"

Jenny Simms was five feet one inch of dark-haired loveliness and fire. Almost, sometimes, the Cactus Kid wished there were less of the fire. At other times, he welcomed it.

The fact that she was the prettiest girl in four counties, that her five feet one inch was firm, shapely, and trim as a two-year-old filly, all conspired to make the Kid cringe at the thought of losing her. He was, unfortunately, in love, and the male animal in love is an abject creature when faced by the tyranny of his beloved. At the time he should be firm, he is weak. At the time he should have been getting her accustomed to driving in harness he was so much in love that he was letting her get the bit in her teeth.

The Cactus Kid, five feet seven inches of solid muscle and bone, curly-haired and given to smiling with a charm all his own, was the most sought-after young man around. At the moment, nobody would have guessed. Nor would they have guessed that the black-holstered, walnut-stocked .44's hanging just now on his saddle were considered by some to be the fastest and deadliest guns in the Rocky Mountain country.

"All right," he said weakly, "I'll get your flowers. Come hell or high water, I'll get 'em!" He gave her his hands and helped her up from the flat rock where she was sitting.

Away from the flashing beauty of Jenny's eyes, he was no longer so confident. Flowers! There wasn't a water hole in fifteen miles that wasn't merely cracked earth and gray mud. The streams had stopped running two months ago. Cattle were dying, all that hadn't been hurriedly sold off, and the leaves on the trees had turned crisp and brown around the edges.

Flowers! He scowled thoughtfully. The Widow Finnegan had a garden, and usually there were flowers in bloom. Now maybe . . .

The piebald gelding with the pink nose and pink-rimmed eyes was a fast horse on the road, and it moved fast now, going through the hills toward the Slash Five and the Widow Finnegan's elm-shaded yard. Yet long before he reached it he could see that even the elms looked parched and bare.

The Widow Finnegan was five feet ten and one hundred and eighty pounds of Irishwoman and she met him at the gate.

"Not here!" She looked about as approachable as a bulldog with a fresh bone. "Not here you don't be gettin' no flowers, Kid!"

"Why, I . . ." His voice trailed away under the pale blue of her glaring eyes.

"There'll be no soft-soapin' me, nayther!" the Widow Finnegan said sharply. "I know the likes of you, Cactus Kid! Full of blarney an' honey-tongued as a thrush! But I know all about the flowers ye'll be wantin', an' there's few enough left, an' them withered!"

"You . . . heard of it?" he asked.

"Heard of it? An' hasn't that colleen o' yours been sayin' all aboot that ye were bringin' her flowers for her birthday! Flowers enough to decorate the rooms with? Flowers in this country where a body is that lucky to find a green blade of grass?"

He glanced thoughtfully at the fence around the small patch of flowers, most of them looking very sick from the hot winds and no rain. She caught his look, and flared.

"No, ye don't! I'm not to be fooled by the likes of ye, Cactus Kid! Ye come back here at night an' every hand on the Slash Five will be digging rock salt out of your southern exposure! An' it's not just talkin' I am!"

A half-dozen men loafed in the High Card Saloon and they all looked up when he shouldered through the door.

"Rye!" he said.

"What's the matter?" Old Man Hawkins leered at him. "Ain't you after the Herrings? Or have they got you buffaloed too?"

The Cactus Kid looked at him with an unfriendly eye. "Got to get some flowers for Jenny," he said lamely, "and she's fussing about me getting into shooting scrapes."

" 'S the way with women," the barkeep said philosophically. "Fall for a man, then set out to change him. Soon's they got him changed they don't like him no more. Never seen it to fail, Kid."

"Speakin' of flowers," Sumner suggested, "I hear tell there's a gent over to Escalante that orders 'em shipped in."

"Be all dried up," the barkeep objected. "Jenny'll want fresh flowers."

"Ain't goin' to find none!" Old Man Hawkins said cheerfully. "Might's well give up, Kid, an' hightail it after the Herrings. You would at least git some money if you got them . . . *if* you got 'em."

The Cactus Kid stared malevolently at his unoffending drink. Meanwhile he tried to arrange his thoughts into some sort of order. Now, flowers. Where would a man be apt to find flowers? Nowhere on the flatland, that was sure. The grass was dried up or the season wrong for any kind he knew of.

A man got up and walked to the bar and stopped beside the Kid. He was a big old man wearing a greasy buckskin shirt.

"I'm Ned Hayes," he said, "prospector. Heard you talkin' about flowers. You'll find plenty in the Blue Mountains. Ain't no drought up thataway. Country shore is green an' purty."

"Thanks." The Kid straightened up, suddenly filled with hope. Then he hesitated, remembering Jenny's admonition about fighting. "Ain't any trouble down thataway, is there? I sure aim to keep out of it this trip."

Hayes chuckled. "Why, man, you won't see a living

soul! Nobody ever goes down there 'cept maybe a drifting
Injun. Robbers' Roost is some north, but they never git
down so far. No, you won't see a soul, but you better pack
extra grub. There's game, but you won't find no cattleman
an' nary a sheep camp. I never seen nobody."

The eight peaks of the mountain group were black
against the sky when the Cactus Kid's first day on the trail
was ending. This was rough, wild, wind-worried and sun-
scorched country, all new to him. Its wild and majestic
beauty was lonely as a plateau on the moon, and water was
scarce. He pushed on, remembering that Ned Hayes had
said there was no drought in the Blues and not wanting to
pitch dry camp out on the escarpment.

"Grassy on the east slopes, Kid," Hayes had added.
"What yuh'll want to do is to cross the Divide. That is, go
over the ridge to the west slope, and there you'll find the
greenest forest you ever saw, rushing mountain streams,
an' a passel of wild flowers of all kinds and shapes."

All day he had seen no track of horse or man, not even
the unshod track of an Indian pony. It was eerie, lonely
country and the Kid found himself glancing uneasily over
his shoulder and staring in awed wonder at the eight
peaks. The mountains were new to him, and they com-
prised a large section of country, all of sixteen miles long
and about ten across.

The piebald was climbing now, and he bent to it with a
will. The Kid had stumbled upon the semblance of a trail,
an ancient Indian route, probably not used in centuries. It
was marked at intervals by small piles of stones such as
used to mark their trails in the deserts farther west.

The horse liked it. He could smell the rich, nutritious
grass, and was ducking his head for an occasional mouth-
ful. He had no idea where this strange master of his was
taking him, but it looked like horse country. Grouse flew
up from under his feet, and once a couple of black-tailed

deer darted away from his movement, then stopped not a dozen yards away to study him.

Before him the hills showed a notch that seemed to offer a pass to the farther side, and the Cactus Kid swung his horse that way. Then he reined in sharply and stared at the ground.

Three hard-ridden horses had cut in sharply from the north, then swung toward the same cut in the hills that he was heading for. And the trail was fresh!

"What d' you know?" the Cactus Kid muttered. "Riders in this country! Well, nothing like company!"

Yet he rode more warily, for well he knew that riders in such an area might be on the dodge. North and west of here was a district in the canyons already becoming famous as Robbers' Roost, and strange bands of horses or cattle occasionally drifted through the country, herded by hard-eyed riders who kept their own counsel and avoided trails.

Chapter II
A Red Herring

Shadows were gathering into black pools in the canyons when he finally saw the notch in the hills deepen into a real opening. The piebald, weary as he was, walked now with his ears cocked forward, and once the Cactus Kid was quite sure he smelled dust in the air.

Despite the heat of the day, the evening grew chill and the night would be cold. The atmosphere was thin here, and the altitude high, yet he wanted to go over the pass before he bedded down. His eyes and ears were alert for sight or sound of the riders who preceded him, but he heard nothing, saw nothing.

At last he rode into the deep shadows of an aspen grove and, hearing water, pushed toward it. Here, on the

banks of a small stream, he found a hollow. He built a fire
carefully shielded, and picketed his horse. After a brief
supper and coffee, he rolled in his blanket and poncho and
slept the night through.

He awoke to find his fire only the soft gray of wood
ashes, the sky of the same shade and texture. Chilled, he
threw off his blankets and built a fire of mountain mahog-
any, young pine, and branches broken from the dead
lower limbs of the aspen. Soon the fire was crackling and
he had water on.

The morning was still and cold. Below him the tops of
trees were like islands in the mist rising from the forest, a
thick fog like the smoke of leaf fires. The air was damp and
the smoke held low, but the hungry tongues of the fire ate
rapidly at the dry branches. In a matter of minutes there
was the smell of coffee and of beef frying.

Several times he walked away from the task of prepar-
ing breakfast to look out through the woods beyond the
hollow in which he was camped. Without any reason, he
felt uneasy and his mind kept returning to the three
riders. No honest men would be in this country unless
they were passing through, and there were easier routes
to the east and north. He thought of the Herrings but
dismissed it at once. They were east of here and by now
the posse probably had them.

His breakfast over, he led the piebald to water, but the
horse refused to drink from the cold stream. Quickly he
saddled up, then mounted. The black-and-white horse
pitched a few times in a casual, disinterested way, more as
a matter of form than of conviction. The Kid moved out.

Almost at once he saw the flowers. Many of them were
sego lilies, faintly orchid in these mountains rather than
pure white. There were other flowers, mostly of purple or
violet colors, shading to white and some to blue. Lilac
sunbonnet, forget-me-not, chia, and many other flowers
seemed to be blooming here, most of which he knew but
slightly or from the Indian use of some of them as reme-
dies or food.

Sighting a particularly thick field of flowers, the Cactus
Kid swung from his saddle and started into the field. He
had stooped to pick flowers when a hard voice spoke
behind him.

"Hold it right there, sprout," the voice said unpleas-
antly, "or you get a Winchester slug in your spine."

The Kid froze, startled but puzzled. "What's the matter?" he asked mildly. "I ain't troubling nobody."

"You ain't goin' to, neither." This was another voice.
"What you doin' here?"

"Came after some flowers for my girl," the Kid said,
realizing as he spoke that it sounded ridiculous.

A big man lumbered around in front of him, glancing
at his face. "Yeah, you're right, Red. It's him. It's the
Cactus Kid, all right. Shucks, I figured him quite a man
from all I heard! This one's only a sprout."

"I don't like that word," the Kid said coldly. "Who are
you, and what do you want with me?"

The big man chuckled. "Hear that, Red? He don't like
being called sprout, an' he's only up here pickin' flowers!
Now, ain't that sweet?"

The man guffawed, then sobered suddenly and struck
the Kid a wicked, backhand blow that knocked him to the
ground. The Kid, fury rising in him and throttling his
good sense, grabbed for his guns. Instantly, a hawk-faced
red-haired man confronted him and there was no arguing
with the rifle in his hands.

"Drop it, Kid! We hear you're mighty fast on the draw,
but you ain't that fast!"

Reluctantly, the Cactus Kid lifted his hands away from
the guns and raised them shoulder high.

"Keep that big lug off me, then," he protested, "or
else take my guns and turn me loose! I'll tear down his
meat house!"

"Why, you dumb sprout!" The big man started forward.
"I got a notion to . . . !"

"Cut it out!" Red said angrily. "What's the matter,
Joe? You lettin' him get your goat? Forget it." The red-

haired man turned his cold gray eyes on the Kid. "Who with you?"

"Nobody! I come up here alone, and like I said, I' after *flowers.*"

"Flowers!" Joe sneered. "He's after flowers! Now wouldn't that kill you? The Cactus Kid, gunfighter ar manhunter, after *flowers!*"

The Kid glared. "I'll peel your hide for this, ye buttonheaded maverick!"

"Shut up!" Red spoke harshly. "Get along toward th dead fir. Right over there! Joe"—Red's voice was sharp "bring that piebald. We can use a good horse."

"You aiming to set me afoot?" The Kid spoke mo quietly. "Look, Red Whatever-your-name-is, I'm on th level about this flower business. My gal down to Helpe she's giving a party. You know how women are."

"How are they?" Red questioned. "I ain't talked to woman in three months. You keep movin', an' watch yo talk to Joe an' Benny. They get mighty touchy."

Joe and Benny . . . and Red.

The Herring brothers!

He was so startled he almost missed his footing an fell, but caught himself in time. Of course! What had h been thinking of not to guess at once who they were? Jo and Benny Herring, killers both of them, wanted for bar and train holdups, but nothing at all to the deadly Re Herring, the gunman from the Gila. A cold-blooded an vicious killer with a flashing speed that had sent more tha one marshal and sheriff to boot hill.

The Herrings . . . and they had him cold turkey. Th boys who had forced a banker to open the bank safe, the escort them from town, and on the outskirts had cooll shot him dead.

And Jenny had warned him against getting into a figh He groaned, and Red Herring prodded him with a rif barrel.

"What's that for?" he demanded.

"Aw, Jenny . . . she's my girl. She warned me not to et in any fights."

Red chuckled without humor. "Don't worry, cowhand, ou ain't in no fight, nor liable to be. You lost this one fore it started. Frankly, we'd as soon hang your hide on he cabin wall as rob a bank. We heard of you."

The Kid decided nothing was to be gained by conver- ation. He had no doubt Red meant just what he said. hey might have had friends, if such men ever had friends, vhom he had gunned down or helped send over the road o the pen. Anyway, in outlaw hangouts the killing of the Cactus Kid would be something to boast about.

Suddenly the earth broke sharply off in a thick grove of spen where a steep, rocky trail wound downward through he trees. It was a one-man-at-a-time trail, and when they eached the bottom they were in a nest of boulders min- led with ancient trees, huge white-limbed deadfalls, and he sound of running water.

Benny Herring was a thin, saturnine man with a scar n his chin. He looked up at them, staring at the Kid.

"He the one followed us?" He stared evilly at the Kid. How'd you spot our trail? Who else knows about it?"

"He says he come up here huntin' flowers!" Joe sneered.

Benny eyed him without humor or interest. "What did ou bring him back for? Why didn't you shoot him an' eave him lay?"

"Buzzards." Red's voice was casual. "Tie him up, Joe."

"Sure." Joe shambled up to him, grinning out of his arrow eyes. Then he smashed the Kid across the face, ver and back, caught him before he fell, and shoved him gainst a stunted tree scarcely taller than the Kid himself.

The Cactus Kid felt blood trickling down his chin, and e glared at Joe, taking a deep breath. Joe tied him tightly nd thoroughly. Then he stared at the Kid, who stared ack at him. Setting himself, Joe hooked a right to his vind and the Kid felt his breath leave him with a gasp.

Without a backward glance, Joe Herring slouched to

the fire and the three began eating, talking in a low
voiced, desultory fashion. Despite their questions about
who else knew of their trail, they seemed unworried, s
the Kid deduced they had actually seen him behind the
on the previous day, and knew he was alone.

He was no fool. His situation was desperate. That the
would not hesitate to leave him dead, he knew. All three
of these men would hang if caught alive and they ha
proved too many times in the past that they had n
hesitation about killing a helpless man. None of them w
the sort to be troubled by qualms or conscience.

Red was obviously the leader, yet from his looks Benn
was no fool. Joe was a hulking brute, physically powerfu
but mentally his range was bare.

The Kid's chances looked nil, and they might kill hi
at any time. However, if they would leave him alone for
while . . . He had his own ideas about that, and his fir
ruse had worked.

Red had said they did not kill him because of buzzard
They were afraid attention might be drawn to the area b
some chance rider seeing circling buzzards. That implie
they were not ready to leave. For all he knew, this are
might be a permanent hideout for them, and might ex
plain why they had so often dropped from sight on prev
ous occasions.

Tentatively, he tried his bonds. Having taken a dee
breath and swelled his muscles before being tied, he no
had a little slack. It was little enough, but he was thankf
that he had not been hit in the wind before being tied, a
that little slack might make all the difference in the worl
His four inches of chest expansion had been a help befor
this, but never had he needed it so much.

His wrists, however, were tightly bound, although h
knew he could move around the tree with some ease if le
alone.

When they finished eating, Benny mounted a hors
and drifted out of the hollow—to act as a lookout, the Ki
guessed. Red smoked a cigarette and eyed the Kid irrita

ly. Obviously, he was in the way, and wouldn't be kept
round for long.

Red Herring was wise in not attracting attention to
heir hideout, for the Cactus Kid knew that searchers
ere not even coming this way, and as this country was
eldom traveled, it was perfection itself for their purposes.
here was small chance that anyone might see the circling
uzzards, but at this time caution was the smart thing and
ed Herring had the cunning of a wolf. At the same time,
he Kid knew that it would serve no purpose to keep him
live. He was only an encumbrance, and the sooner they
d themselves of him the better off they were.

An idea came to the Kid suddenly, an idea that might
eep him alive a little longer, and he desperately wanted
o live.

"You got it mighty good here," he said. "Only that
oney won't do you much good in this hole."

"We don't aim to stay." Red threw a couple of dry
ticks on the fire. "Just to let things quiet down."

"They'll be watching for you at Hanksville, Green-
iver, and Dandy Crossing. At Helper and Henrieville,
oo."

Herring looked up, studying the Kid. "How'd you
now that?"

"They wanted me in the posse. I wouldn't go because
hy girl wanted the flowers."

Red grunted. "You stickin' to that story? Why come
ay down here?"

"Figure it out for yourself. With this drought there
in't none anywhere around. Prospector told me about
hese flowers. Hombre name of Hayes."

Red nodded. "Know about him. So they got us bottled
p, have they? Why tell us? Why not let us ride into a
rap?"

The Kid grinned wryly. "Because I want to live. To get
ou killed after I'm dead doesn't help me, and the way I
gure it, you don't aim to let me live that long."

"That's right. We'll kill you before the day's out. Drop

you in a hole over west of here. Still, I don't see why y
tell me."

"I said, because I want to live . . . and there's a w
out of this country."

"Out of here? How?" The Kid was aware of Rec
awakened interest. If he could keep him hooked . . .

"South of here, if you know the water holes. Othe
wise, you can die out there."

"South?" Red studied the situation. "That's a migh
long ride. I heard a man couldn't make it through. Y
know the water holes?"

"Sure, I know 'em. And I know the trails like an Inju
You boys aren't known down thataway, either, are you?"

Red got to his feet and walked over, rolling a smok
He stuck the cigarette in the Kid's lips and lit it.

"No, we ain't." He studied the Kid carefully. "Y
figure we'll let you go if you take us through?"

The Kid grinned. "No. I never heard of you doir
anybody any favors, Red. But the longer I stay alive tl
better my chances are. You might decide to lay off, or
might get a chance to light a shuck."

Red chuckled but without humor. "Yeah, that's reasor
able enough. You're buying time."

Chapter III
Desperate Chance

Nothing more was said and they waited the hours out. Th
men changed jobs from time to time, and there was muc
low-voiced discussion among them. As the night drew o
it became rapidly colder. At dusk Benny came in fro
watching and the three ate, talked longer, then rolled u
in their blankets and went to sleep.

The Cactus Kid shivered in the cold, crisp air, h
body held immobile by his bonds. He tried tensing grou

of muscles to keep his circulation alive and ward off the worst of the cold, and after a while he tried his bonds. The four inches of chest expansion had given him a little slack with which to work, and he could turn his body on the dead tree. Yet for all his straining he could do little with the rawhide thongs that bound his hands behind him.

Morning dawned cold and crisp and Benny walked over to him and untied him. "Set and eat," he said briefly.

For an hour they questioned him about the route south, and his answers evidently satisfied them. Much of this country was as strange to him as to them, but he did know that trail out, and he was sure that once they were traveling, his chance would come. Anyway, it was a reprieve, if only for a few days.

After having him collect more wood while watched by Joe with a rifle, they tied him again, and this time left him sitting on the ground. This time, too, he held his breath and bulged his muscles while straining for slack. And again he got it, although not so much as before.

Red was the first guard and he walked away from camp right away. Benny returned to the Kid and plied him with questions about the trail. He seemed disturbed by the trip, but why, the Cactus Kid could not gather.

Then, almost at noon, Red came in leading the horses. "We'll go," he said. "Nobody's coming. Far's a man can see, that trail's empty. We've lost 'em, but to go out thataway would be asking for trouble. The Kid can guide us over this south trail."

Although his weapons were carried by Joe Herring, the Cactus Kid was left unbound. At once, he headed off south through the mountains with Red beside him and the other Herrings immediately behind. Leaving the hills, they descended to Sage Plain, skirted Elk Ridge and the Bear's Ears, dropped into Cottonwood Wash and proceeded along it and then out into a fantastic world of eerie towers and spires like the images of cathedrals cast in stone.

At dark, he brought them up to a spring, a small

trickle of water running from a fracture in the rock into a
small basin, which overflowed in turn to be lost in the
sand. Nearby were several windbreaks made by Indians
from pine boughs or slabs of rock. There was no evidence
of human life other than that, and no sign that anybody
had been near in months.

Once, on the rim of a canyon, Red Herring drew up
sharply.

"Thought you said there was nobody down thisaway?"

"What do you see?" the Kid asked curiously.

"House, or building over yonder." Herring stood in his
stirrups and squinted. "Sort of tower."

"Oh, that?" The Kid shrugged. "Injun ruins. Lots of
them down here." He turned the piebald down a steep
trail to the canyon bottom. Here, in this well-watered
place, they rode into groves of fir, pine, and black balsam,
while snowberry and manzanita grew thick along the canyon walls. There was grass, and yet here and there clumps
of desert plants had invaded this richer, moister soil.

Late in the afternoon Red Herring suddenly snapped
his rifle to his shoulder. Its report bellowed against the
canyon walls and a mule deer plunged to its knees, tried
to get up, then sprawled out.

"Nothing like fresh meat," Red said with satisfaction.

"Who skins it?" Joe demanded belligerently. "Why
don't we make this sprout work?" He grinned at the Kid.
"Let him earn his keep."

"Good idea," Red said, "you're cook from here on,
Kid."

"Good!" the Cactus Kid said. "Now I can get some
decent chuck for a while. That Joe cooks like he was fixing
food for hogs."

Joe glared, and Benny chuckled. "Danged if it ain't the
truth!" he said. "He had you there, Joe!"

Accepting the knife tossed to him, the Kid got busy
over the deer, cutting out some fine steaks. As he worked,
he was thinking swiftly. This might be the gamble he
wanted, and in any event, it was worth taking a chance. As

he gathered fuel for the fire and started his broiling of the steaks, he thought rapidly.

Back along the line there had been some desert brush, among them a plant he had recognized. It was a low-growing shrub, without leaves at this time of year, but with its stems dotted with odd, glandlike swellings. As he worked, the Kid kept his eyes busy and finally located the plant he sought, a relative of the rue known in many lands or medicinal effects. Carefully, from under the plant he gathered some of the dried leaves and, when making coffee, crushed a double handful and dropped them into the boiling water with the coffee. Finding more of the plants, he gathered a stack of the leaves while collecting wood and put them down not far from the fire.

Red bit into his first piece of steak, then looked up at the Kid. "You just got yourself a few more days, podner. This is *grub*!"

Even the surly Joe agreed that the Cactus Kid could cook, but when he tasted the coffee, he stared at it.

"Tastes funny," he said, scowling.

Red picked up his cup and tried it. "Tastes good to me," he said. "It's just that your taster has been tuint by that alkali and coffee junk you put out for coffee."

The Kid added more fuel to the fire. Soon they would tie him, but how soon? He had to guess right and beat them to it. Whether his stunt would work, he did not know, but it was a gamble he had to take. The Utes had told him of the plant and its effects, that it was used by them as a sedative, and that leaves thrown on a fire provided undisturbed sleep.

He poured a liberal cup of coffee for himself, but he managed to see that his cup came only after they had been served, and from a second batch that contained none of the leaves. Getting up, the Kid threw some more brush on the fire, and with it the small mound of leaves he had gathered. They burned slowly, and the smoke grew thicker, but the aroma was not unpleasant.

Benny looked up suddenly. "Joe, you better tie him up. I'm getting sleepy."

"Me too," Red agreed. "That was a long ride, and I ate more'n usual."

Joe Herring lumbered to his feet. Crossing to the Kid, he jerked his wrists behind him and tied them together, his fingers clumsy with sleep. Then he tied the Kid's feet together and walked back to his bedroll.

Red was already asleep, his blanket pulled over him. At the fire, Benny dozed, and while the Cactus Kid watched hopefully, smoke drifted across his face and the man nodded. Finally, with a glance over at the Kid, Benny got up and went to his bedroll. And then, for a long time, there was silence.

The Kid was working hard. His breath coming hoarsely, he struggled with the poorly tied thongs on his wrists. Unable to do much with them, he hooked the toes of his boots under a log and carefully, with much struggling, succeeded in drawing his feet out of the boots. Then he backed around to them and managed to dig their toes down into the sand so that he could rub the rawhide on the rowels of his spurs. It took him more than an hour and then the thongs dropped free and he drew his wrists from behind him. They were chafed and bloody, but free!

Sitting perfectly still, he worked his fingers to restore circulation, then removed the thongs from around his boots and put them on. Crossing to the stack of guns, he picked up his own and belted them on, then put his rifle carefully to one side and considered the situation.

The Herrings were not doped. Not, at least, to the extent that they had passed out. From what he had heard the qualities of the plant he had used were sufficient only to induce a sound sleep, which, added to their natural drowsiness from the long day in the saddle and warm food, had been sufficient. Yet he was sure that the slightest sound of a squabble and they would awaken.

Knowing them, he knew they would come awake fighting. They would gamble. Whether he could manage without awakening them he did not know, and his first instinct was for flight. Yet here they were, the men wanted so badly, and the reward would do a lot toward stocking a ranch as well as removing from circulation some badmen no better than mad dogs.

Red was sleeping with his guns on and his rifle beside him. Benny had been more careless, yet his weapons were close. Joe, who had been carrying the Kid's weapons, had left them all together.

Moving carefully out of camp, the Kid got the piebald and saddled him. When he was ready, in case of emergency, the Kid walked slowly back to camp. Very gently, he slipped a loop over Joe's wrists and drew it as tight as he dared. The big man was sleeping with his knees drawn up, so the Kid bound his wrists down to his knees. He was just straightening up when, lifting his eyes, he looked into the startled, staring eyes of Ben Herring!

Instantly, Ben yelled. "Red! Look out! The Kid's loose!" And at the same instant he grabbed for his gun.

"Drop it!" The Cactus Kid's gun leaped into his hand. "Drop!"

Ben's finger whitened on the trigger and the Kid's gun bellowed. It was point-blank range and a fast shot. The bullet hit the cartridges in Ben's belt and glanced, smashing his elbow. The thin man dropped his gun and grabbed his arm, while on the ground Joe thrashed around, trying to free himself.

A gun bellowed from the brush and the Kid dove for shelter among some rocks. Red had not waited to draw iron, but had leaped instantly for shelter. Now he crouched there across the fire, and the Cactus Kid knew he was in for the fight of his life.

"Quiet down, Joe," the Kid called, "or I'll put a slug in you!"

Joe ceased struggling and Ben sat there by the fire, gripping his bloody arm. "I'm out of this! You crippled me!"

"See you stay out of it!" the Kid replied shortly. Then he faded back into the deeper darkness.

He was desperately worried. The night was intensely dark, and he knew from his own moving around that a man could move easily and make no sound. The trees were not too close together, and the clumps of brush could be avoided. And Red Herring was a killer, a man with every sense alert, knowing that if captured he would hang.

Moreover, the man would be filled with hatred now, and the Kid knew he had never faced a man more dangerous, more filled with concentrated evil and malice than Red Herring.

Chapter IV
Jenny's Party

The Cactus Kid lay still, well back from the fire. He knew that every second he was out of sight of the camp was a second fraught with even greater danger, for if they realized he was gone, Ben would free Joe and he would be facing two men and possibly a third.

There was no sound. The darkness lay thick and still around him. The stars were lost above a cushion of thick cloud; there was no wind. Somewhere a stone rattled, but it was far away. The Kid began to sweat. His stomach felt hollow and he stared, straining his eyes into the darkness, fighting down his desire to move, to get away from there. Yet to move might mean death, and his best plan was not to move, but to lie still, to force Red to come to him. And he knew that Red Herring, outlaw and murderer, would do just that.

One of the horses stamped, and somewhere a grouse called into the night. The Cactus Kid shifted his gun and dried his sweaty palm on his shirt. Ever so carefully, the

Kid moved, sliding his body along the ground, edging toward a clump of manzanita that would permit a view of the fire.

Ben was fighting to bind his arm, and Joe was cursing steadily, staring toward the outer circle of darkness. The Kid waited, and an hour went slowly by.

Suddenly, he stiffened with realization. While he waited, tense with watching for Red, who would be stalking him, the fire was dying!

With the fire dead, and the two men in the circle of its light freed from his watching eyes, he would lose control over the situation and at once he would become the hunted, not the hunter!

Yet he dared not call out to order them to build the fire. To speak would be to have his position riddled with bullets. Cold in the blackness, he fought for a solution, and then, suddenly, he had what seemed to be the answer.

The loot.

It lay almost halfway around the circle, on the edge of the firelight. Soon the place where it lay would be in darkness. Probably as soon as he could get to it. Lying there, forgotten in the face of more immediate problems, it could be the key to the whole show. If he could get the money, then get to his horse, he might at least save the loot. And he might succeed in drawing the Herrings into a trap. For if he had the money, they would follow him.

Slowly, inch by inch, he worked his way along the ground, circling the fire. At any instant he might come face to face with Red; at any instant they might shoot it out. And over there in the circle of trees, the fire was flickering only in a few spots now.

Then the sacks of loot were there, only a short distance from his hands. With infinite care, he reached out and lifted them one by one back into the brush. Fortunately, there was little gold, so the weight was nothing to worry about. With the sacks in his left hand he eased back and got to his feet.

He found the piebald by his white spots and moved to

him. The horse sidestepped and instantly the area flame with light! A gun bellowed and a shot plucked at hi sleeve.

Red Herring, guessing he would come for the saddle horse, had waited beside a stack of dry brush covered wit leaves!

The flare of the fire, the stab of the shot, and his ow action were one. Flinging himself in a long dive, the Ki went, not for shelter or for the horse, but straight at th stabbing flame of the shot!

A gun roared again and he heard the slam of the sho past his ear and then he was in the brush. Red Herrin sprang to his feet and triggered the gun at point-blan range, but the Kid was coming too hard, and as he fired Herring tried to step back. A rock rolled under his foo and his shot missed, and then the Cactus Kid hit him wit his pistol.

Herring staggered, then caught himself and swun wickedly with the barrel of his gun for the Kid's head but, rolling over, the Cactus Kid smashed his bod against Herring's legs and the cursing outlaw wer down.

Both men came up without guns and the Cactus Kic fighting with the madness of fear, realizing his tim was short, slashed into the outlaw with both fists wing ing. His right caught Herring on the jaw and knocke him into a tree, and before Red could set himsel the Cactus Kid closed in, smashing left and right t the head, a smashing right to the body, and a wicke left that broke Herring's nose and showered him wit blood. Herring swung, missed, and his chin blocke a wicked right with all the Kid's lean, muscular powe behind it. Herring hit the sand flat on his face an the Kid dove for his gun even as Joe and Ben cam plowing through the brush.

"Freeze!" The Kid's gun was on them. "Drop 'em boys, or I'll plant all of you right here!" He had the dro . . . and they let go their guns.

• • •

It was midafternoon, four days later. The town was crowded with the Saturday flux of ranchers. Suddenly, there was a startled yell, and men poured into the streets.

Down the dusty main drag came four riders. Three rode abreast, and all who saw them immediately recognized the three bloody Herrings. Joe, who rode on the right, had a huge armful of sego lilies, as did Ben, who rode on the left. Red, who rode in the middle, his horse carefully roped to the other two, carried a huge armful of western forget-me-nots and purple verbena mingled with a few bunches of lilac sunbonnets.

The town stared, then it cheered, and the Herrings glowered. Up the street they went, followed by the crowd, and halted before the Simms's home.

"Oh, Nesselrode! You're *wonderful*! You got my flowers!"

"Yeah." He dismounted stiffly and began taking the flowers from the arms of the three surly outlaws. Red's head was wrapped in a bloody bandage torn from a shirt. Ben's arm was in a sling.

"Got 'em. Better get 'em in water. They may be wilted some."

If Jenny noticed the Herrings it was not obvious. "Oh, Nesselrode! I knew you could do it! I just *knew* you could!"

Joe Herring glowered. "Huh! Nesselrode! Kotched by an hombre name of *Nesselrode*!"

The Cactus Kid turned and his eyes were deadly. "I never shot a man with his hands tied, but you mention that name again and you'll be the first!"

The sheriff came pounding up with two deputies and took the prisoners.

"Well, what do you know, Jenny!" he exclaimed. "This cowpuncher of yours caught the Herring boys!"

"The Herring boys?" She smiled prettily. "Oh, Sheriff, will you ask your wife to come over and help me decorate? I don't know whether that verbena would go better in the parlor or—"

The sheriff bit off a chew.

"You catch the three meanest outlaws west of the Rockies," he said to the Kid, "and she wants to know whether the verbena will look better in one room or t'other!" He spat. "Women! I never will get 'em figured out!"

The Cactus Kid grunted, and dug out the makings. He was unshaven and the desert dust was thick on his clothes. He was half dead from his long ride and lack of sleep.

Jenny appeared suddenly in the door. "Oh, Nesselrode? Will you help me a minute, please? Pretty please?"

The Kid looked at the sheriff, and the sheriff shrugged. "Yeah," the Kid said, low-voiced. Then he looked up. "Coming, honey!" he said.

The
Ghost Maker

Author's Note

In the early days of riding and ranching, very few of the horses were more than half broken. And likely they would start bucking the moment a cowboy swung his leg over the saddle. Consequently, he wanted that pointed toe of his boot to slip easily into the stirrup, and the high heel to prevent slipping too far.

The usual practice was to bring horses in off the range to one fellow in the outfit, usually one who was a pretty good rider, who would do what they call "break the rough string." He would saddle up these unbroken horses and ride them until they stopped pitching, and that horse was considered broken.

The animal would be left there for the next cowboy to have his own little time with him, because very few of the cowboys liked a horse that wouldn't buck. And most of them did buck in the morning, especially when it was frosty.

A thoughtful rider always took his bit to the fire and warmed it some before he put it in the horse's mouth. Or sometimes he'd get it warm by wearing it inside his shirt for a while.

M arty Mahan, tall in the saddle of his black gelding, rode in the Grand Entry Parade of the Wind River Annual Rodeo, but beside him rode fear. Tall and splendidly built, clad in silver and white, Mahan was a fine-looking rider, and the crowd, which looked down to applaud, and to whose applause he responded with a wave of his Stetson, knew he was one of the greatest riders the West had seen.

For two years he had won top honors in the Wind River show. At a dozen other rodeos he was considered, by performers as well as spectators, one of the finest all-round cowboys riding the tanbark. Yet today fear rode with him, and hatred and contempt rode beside him. The fear was in the memory of a day and a horse; the hatred was in the person of big Yannell Stoper, the hard-faced roughneck of the contests, who rode beside him in the parade.

"How does it feel, Pretty Boy?" Yannell sneered. "How does it feel to know you're through? You know what they'll say when they find out? You're yellow! Yellow, Mahan! Just as yellow as they come! That Ghost Maker will show 'em today! You mark my words!"

Mahan said nothing, his face stiff and white. There was too much truth in what Stoper was saying. He was afraid—he had always been afraid of Ghost Maker.

Yannell Stoper had reason to know. Three times hand running, three years before, Marty Mahan had beaten

Yannell out for top money, and Stoper was not a man wh
took losing lightly. His animosity for Mahan developed
but he had detected no flaw in the other rider until tha
day at Twin Forks.

It was a small rodeo, just a fill-in for riders of th
stamp of Stoper and Mahan, and neither of them ha
figured on much trouble. Marty had won the calf ropin
without even extending himself, and Stoper had taken th
steer wrestling easily. Both riders had allowed the lesse
names to come in for money in other events, pointin
themselves at the bronc riding.

Marty Mahan had been his usual devil-may-care se
until the names of the riders and their mounts were posted
Marty Mahan was posted as riding Ghost Maker.

"What a name!" he said, grinning. "I wonder wh
thinks them up?"

Red Blade shrugged. "This one deserves his name!" h
said wryly. "You should do top money if you top off tha
horse! He earned his name up in Calgary!"

"Calgary?" Yannell noticed a subtle change in Mahan'
voice, and had turned to watch him. "This Ghost Make
from up there?"

"Sure is!" Blade spat. "Killed a man up there tw
seasons ago. Mighty fine rider, too. Man by the name e
Cy Drannan. Throwed him an' then tromped him to death
Caught him in his teeth, flung him down, then lit in wit
all four feet! He's a reg'lar devil!"

"A big zebra dun?" Marty asked. Stoper recalled after
ward that it had seemed less a question than a statement

"That's right! An' pure poison!"

Marty Mahan was taken suddenly ill and could no
ride. Yannell Stoper thought that one over, and curiousl
he watched both Marty and the dun horse. Mahan ha
come out to see the bronc riding, but he seemed pale an
hollow-eyed. Yannell studied him shrewdly and decide
that Mahan was sick all right, sick with fear. He wa
afraid, deathly afraid of the big dun!

And Ghost Maker did his best to live up to his name

Bud Cameron asked for the horse when Marty could not ride. Bud was thrown, lasting scarcely two seconds on the hurricane deck of the squealing, sunfishing devil of a dun. He hit the ground in a heap and staggered to his feet. Amid the roar of the crowd. Mahan leaped up, screaming!

His voice was lost in the thunder of shouting, lost to all but Stoper, who was watching the man he hated. He saw that scream was a scream of fear, but of warning, too! For the zebra dun, neck stretched and teeth bared, knocked the puncher sprawling and lit into him with both feet. They got the maddened animal away from the fallen man, but before nightfall the word was around. Bud Cameron would never ride again. He would never walk again. He was crippled for life.

Big, tawny, lion-headed Yannell Stoper had no thought of Bud Cameron. The breaks of the game. What he did think about was Marty Mahan, for Marty was afraid. He was afraid of Ghost Maker. It was something to remember.

At Prescott and Salinas, Mahan beat Stoper out for top money, but Ghost Maker was not around. He was piling riders down in Texas and killing his second man. Stoper made sure that Marty knew about that. After Marty won at Salinas, Yannell congratulated him.

"Lucky for you it wasn't the Ghost Maker," Yannell said. Mahan's head came up, his face gone pale. "I see he killed another man down in Texas!"

Mahan, his face white, had walked away without speaking. Behind him, Yannell had smiled grimly. This was something to know.

Yannell Stoper had his own ideas about men. A man who was afraid of anything was a man who was yellow. It was just in him, that was all. He did not know that a man who can face fists is often deathly afraid of a gun, and that a gunman may shrink from the cold steel of a knife. Or a man of utmost cowardice before some kinds of danger may face another kind with high courage. To Yannell Stoper a man who was yellow was yellow, and that was final. And

to his satisfaction, Marty Mahan was yellow. It was a fact
to be remembered and to be used.

Yannell Stoper was big, rugged, and rough. In a lifetime of battling with hard broncs and harder men he had
rarely known defeat, and never known fear. He had nothing but contempt for men who were afraid of anything, or
who admitted doubt of themselves in any situation that
demanded physical courage.

Now, on this day at the Wind River Rodeo, Yannell
Stoper was ready for his triumph. It was a triumph that
would mean much to him, one he had carefully engi-
neered. For it was at Stoper's suggestion that the contest
officials had secured the string of rough buckers of which
the Ghost Maker was one.

Here in Wind River, before the world of the rodeo and
the eyes of Peg Graham he would expose the cowardice of
Marty Mahan for all the world to see.

"He's here!" Yannell taunted. "Right here in Wind
River, an' if you duck ridin' him here they'll all know
you're yellow!"

They would, too! Even Marty had heard, or rather,
overheard, the stories. He knew Stoper had started them
himself, planting the seeds for the exposure, removing at
once his rival for top rodeo honors and for Peg Graham.

"They say Mahan will drop out rather than ride Ghost
Maker," a big rancher had said the evening before. "He's
scared of the hoss! Dropped out of a show down in Texas
rather than tackle him!"

"He's a bad horse," Red Carver admitted, "but you
never make a good ride on an easy one!"

Marty had turned away and walked back toward the
hotel, sick and ashamed. For he was afraid. He had been
afraid of Ghost Maker from the day he had first seen him
on that lonely Nevada range where he had run wild. He
had been afraid of him ever since he had seen the dun lift

is head, nostrils flared, and then come mincing toward im, walking so quietly away from the herd.

A wild horse that did not run. That should have warned im, and if it had not, the reaction of his own mount would have, for his horse began to quiver and edge away, lowing with fright. An old rancher had told Marty once, Kill him the second he shows he's a killer, or he'll get ou sure!"

Real man-killers were rare, but there was in them omething of a fiend, of a destroying demon that came on o gently, then charged with wide jaws and flaring eyes. And Ghost Maker was such a horse, a horse marked from irth with a vicious hatred of man or even of other horses, f anything that moved and was not of his own herd.

Mahan had been seventeen at the time he first glimpsed he Ghost Maker. He had felt his horse shy, felt the quivering fright in the animal. Marty was younger then nd he was curious. Above all, this wild horse seemed so ame, so friendly.

Suddenly the dun had darted at them, frenzied with illing fury. In a flash he had struck down Mahan's saddle orse. Marty had fallen free and the dun had rushed at im, but the effort of his gray to get off the ground istracted the maddened horse, and the stallion had wheeled nd struck wickedly at the gray. Fighting like a very fiend ncarnate, the zebra dun had attacked the gray horse and truck and slashed until the saddle horse was a bloody eap of dead flesh, hammered, chopped, and pounded ntil all life was gone and even the saddle was a ruined nd useless thing.

Marty, crouching weaponless between two boulders, vatched that holocaust of butchery with horror-stricken yes, unable to do anything to protect the old saddle horse e had ridden. And then, his killing fury unabated, the un had come for him, lunging with slashing hoofs at the ocks, but unable because of the position in which he lay, o get at the boy.

For three fear-haunted hours the killer dun had circle
those rocks. Time and again he struggled to get at the bo
lying in the crevice. In those hours had been born a
overwhelming horror of the horse. A horror that was neve
forgotten. Long after the horses had gone, led away by th
dun on some whim of the wild, Marty had lain there
cramped and still, fearing to move, fearing to show himse
in the open where the stallion might again come upo
him.

Never again had he gone up on the range without
pistol, but never again had he gone to that section of th
range. He had seen no more of the horse until that day i
Calgary when the dun had shown itself under the saddl
of Cy Drannan, Marty's best friend. Marty had hurried t
the rider and told him the horse was a killer.

"So what?" Drannan shrugged. "I've heard of killer
but never seen one! I always figured I'd like to top on
off!"

Cy Drannan, happy, friendly, a good companion an
rider, died on the bloody tanbark that day under th
lashing hoofs of a horse that was a cunning, hate-ridde
devil.

Now that horse was here, in this show, and *he* was t
ride him. He, Marty Mahan.

Peg Graham was waiting for him when the parad
ended. Her eyes were bright.

"Oh, Marty! Dad's said that after the rodeo if yo
will buy that Willow Creek range he will give his cor
sent!"

Marty nodded soberly. "Does it have to be right away
honey?" he asked. "I mean, I . . . well, I may not mak
enough money in this show. Added to what I have, it wi
have to be a good fifteen hundred to swing that deal. I'
have to win four events to make it."

"Not if you win the bronc riding, Marty! They've uppe
the prize money and have offered a flat thousand dollar

r top money! You can win it! You've already beaten both
ed Carver and Yannell Stoper before!"

He hesitated, his face flushing. "I'm not riding broncs
this show, Peg," he said slowly. "I'm going to go in for
alf roping, bull riding, steer wrestling, and some other
uff, but not bronc riding."

Peg Graham's face had turned a shade whiter, and her
yes widened. "Then . . . then it's true what they say! You
re afraid!"

He looked at her, then glanced away, his heart misera-
le within him. "Yeah, I guess I am," he said, "I guess I
m afraid of that horse!"

Peg Graham stared at him, "Marty, I'll never marry a
oward! I'll never have it said that my man was afraid to
de a horse that other men would ride! Red Carver has
ked for that horse! Yannell says—"

"Yannell?" Marty looked at the girl. "You've been talk-
g to him?"

"Yes, I have!" she flashed. "At least, he's not afraid of a
orse!" She turned on her heel and walked swiftly away,
very inch of her quivering with indignation.

Mahan started to turn, then stopped. And old man with
drooping yellowed mustache leaned against the corral.

"Tough, kid!" he said. "I didn't aim to overhear, but
uldn't help it. You up to ride the Ghost Maker?"

Marty nodded. "I'm not ridin' him, though!" he said.
That horse is a devil! He shouldn't be allowed in shows
ke this! That isn't sport or skill. . . . It's plain, unadulter-
ed murder!"

"Reckon I agree with you," the old timer said seri-
usly. "It ain't a bit smart to tackle a horse like that! I've
en him in action, an' he's a killer all through!"

Marty nodded unhappily. "He's from my home range
the Black Rock Desert country. He killed my ridin'
orse once, about five years ago."

"You Marty Mahan?" the old man inquired. "I'm Old
hn. Heard a lot about you. You don't look like no
oward."

Marty's eyes flashed. "I'm not! But I am afraid of th horse! I'm not aimin' to fool anybody about that!"

"Takes a good man to admit he's scared," Old Joh commented thoughtfully. "Who rides him if you don't?"

"Carver an' Stoper both want him. I wish they'd leav him out of this. He's a killer and a devil. There's som thing in that horse that ain't right."

"Like some men I know," John agreed. "There's kille in all sorts of critters. Just got a streak of meanness a devil in 'em." He hitched up his pants. "Well, luck to yo son. I'll be amblin'."

Marty Mahan stared after the old man, his brow fu rowed. He had never seen *him* around before.

The memory of Peg's face cut him like a knife. Sh believed him a coward. . . . Well, maybe he was! H walked over to Jeff Allen, chairman of the rodeo committee

"Jeff, I'm withdrawin' from the bronc ridin'. I wor ride that Ghost Maker."

Allen shifted his cigar in his jaws. "Heard you didr aim to. You say he's a killer?"

"He sure is." Briefly, Marty related his own exper ences with the horse. "Personally, I think you should tal him out of the lists."

Jeff Allen shook his head. His cold blue eyes showe disdain. "Not a chance! Just because you're afraid to tack him don't mean others won't! Stoper has been arour here, beggin' for him!"

Marty saw nothing of Peg Graham, nor of her fathe Alone, he waited by the chutes for the calf roping, whic was the first event in which he was entered. None of th rodeo hands stopped near him, nor did the contestant Bitterly, his heart heavy in his chest, he watched the and watched the crowd. Once, over beyond the corral h saw Peg Graham. She was with Yannell Stoper.

Stoper opened in the calf roping and made a qui chase, a clean catch, and a fast tie. It was good time. Re

Carver and Bent Wells fell a little short. Marty Mahan's black was a darting flash when the calf left the pens. He swept down his rope streaking like a thrown lance. The catch was perfect and he hit the ground almost as the rope tightened. He dropped his calf, made his tie, and straightened to his feet, his hands in the air.

"Folks!" Roberts boomed. "That's mighty fast time! Marty Mahan, internationally famous rodeo star, makes his tie in eleven and two-tenths seconds!"

Three-tenths of a second better than Stoper. Marty turned, amid cheers, toward his black horse, and then somebody—and away down within him Marty was sure it was Stoper—yelled:

"Where's the Ghost Maker? Get Ghost Maker!"

The crowd took it up, and as Marty cantered from the arena his ears rang with the taunting word.

"Get Ghost Maker! Let him ride Ghost Maker! *Yellow!*"

White-faced, he dropped to the ground. Old John looked up at him.

"Hard to take, ain't it, boy?"

Mahan did not reply, but his face was pale and set. Yannell Stoper came around the corral, several riders with him.

"There's the hero! Wants milk-wagon horses!"

Marty turned sharply. "That will be enough of that!" he snapped.

Yannell halted, astonished. Then his eyes narrowed. "Why, you yeller-bellied, white-livered son—!"

They started for each other, fists clenched. The loudspeaker boomed out.

"Stoper! Ready for steer wrestling! Stoper! On your horse!"

With a curse the big tawny-headed man turned. "Saved you from a beatin'!" he sneered. "You get the breaks!"

"See me later, then!" Marty flashed back at him. "Anywhere! Any time!"

Grimly, he walked away. Behind him he heard the roar of the crowd as Yannel went after his steer. For a

minute Marty Mahan stood still, listening to that ro..
behind him. Soon he would be going out there, facing th..
crowd again, and they would taunt and boo again. It w..
no use. . . . Why bother? He might as well quit now!

Then another thought came and he stopped in midstrid..
Run? Like the devil he would! He'd go back there an..
make them eat their taunts. Every word! He wheeled an..
walked back. When the time came for him to go out h..
went like a demon, flashing with speed. He took his ste..
down faster than ever before in his life, and as the lou..
speaker boomed out his time, he swung into the saddle.

Taunts and jeers burst from the stands, but this tin..
instead of riding out, he rode over before the stands an..
sat there, his hat lifted in salute. As the yells, boos, an..
hisses swept the arena, he sat perfectly still, his fac..
dead-white, his eyes bright, waiting for stillness. It cam..
at last. Then he waved his hat once more and, turning h..
horse, walked him quietly from the arena, leaving dea..
silence behind him.

Old John stood beside Peg Graham, who watched, h..
eyes wide. "That," Old John commented dryly, "too..
sand!"

She turned quickly to look at him. Then her eyes wer..
back to the man riding from the area. "I . . . guess it did..
she agreed hesitantly. Her brows puckered. "I don't kno..
you, do I?"

Old John rolled his quid in his jaws. "No, ma'am, yc..
don't. Nor a real man when you see him!" He turne..
abruptly and walked off, leaving the girl's face flushin..
with embarrassment and shame.

As she turned away, she wondered. Had she wronge..
Marty Mahan? Was he a coward because he refused..
ride that horse? If a man went into contest riding, he w..
not expected to be afraid of bad horses. He was expecte..
to ride anything given him. Mostly the riders wanted ba..
horses because it gave them the best chance to make..
good ride. Even if this horse was as bad as Mahan claime..
was it reason for refusing?

In the last analysis, she guessed it was simply that she could not bear to have him called a coward, or to love a man who was yellow.

Yannell Stoper won the bareback bronc riding in both the first and second go-rounds. Then he appeared in his usual exhibition of trick riding, and the first day of the rodeo ended with Stoper as the hero of the show despite his loss to Marty in the calf roping. His insistence on riding the horse that Mahan refused caught the crowd's interest.

Mahan was disconsolate. He walked the streets, feeling singularly out of place in his expensive trappings, and wishing he were miles away. Only the knowledge that if he left the show he would be branded a quitter, and through in the arena, kept him in town. That and the fascination exerted over him by the dun horse.

As the evening drew on he heard more and more talk of the dun. Despite their willingness to call him a coward for refusing the horse, people were beginning to wonder if the animal were not a killer after all. At all these rumors Yannell scoffed.

Marty Mahan was at supper when the café door slammed open and big, tawny-haired Stoper came in with Red Carver and Peg Graham. When the girl saw Marty sitting at the table alone she would have turned to leave, but Yannell would have none of it. They trooped in and, with several hangers-on, seated themselves at tables near Mahan's. At the counter not far away sat Old John, calmly eating doughnuts and drinking coffee.

"Sure I'll ride him!" Stoper boomed loudly. "I'm not yellow! I'll ride anything that wears hair!"

Mahan looked up. Inside he was strangely still and at ease. It was only his mind that seemed suddenly white-hot, yet his eyes were clear and hard. He looked across at Yannell Stoper and their eyes met.

"Finally got showed up, didn't you?" Stoper sneered. "You was always a four-flusher!"

"And you were always a loudmouth," Marty said quietly.

Stoper's face flushed red. Then his blue-white eye
narrowed down and he began to smile. He pushed bac
from the table.

"I always wanted to get my hands on you and in jus
about a minute I'll slap all the coward to the surface!"

He got up and started around the table. Carver calle
to him, and Peg Graham got up, her hand going to he
mouth, eyes wide and frightened.

"And in just about a half minute," Marty said, slidin
out of his chair, "you'll wish you'd never opened you
mouth!"

Stoper walked in smiling and when he got to arm'
length, he swung. It was a powerful, wide-armed punch
but Mahan's left shot straight from the shoulder to Stop
er's mouth, setting the big rider back on his heels. The
Marty crossed with a smashing right that dropped Yanne
to his haunches.

Mahan stepped back, his face calm. "If you want t
ride that horse tomorrow," he said, "you'd better save it!"

Stoper came up with a lunge and dove for Marty, wh
stepped into a chair and tripped. Before he could regai
his balance, Stoper was on him with a smashing volley o
punches. Mahan staggered and Yannell was all over him
his face set in a mask of fury, his punches smashing an
driving. Yet somehow Mahan weathered the storm, cov
ered and got in close. Grabbing Yannell by the belt wit
one hand and a knee with the other, he upended th
furious puncher and dropped him to the floor.

Stoper came up with a growl of rage and Mahan smashe
a left and right to the face. The left went to the mouth, t
Stoper's already bleeding lips, and showered him wit
blood. Marty stepped to the side and avoided a right, the
countered with a wicked right to the wind. Yannell gaspe
and Mahan stabbed a left, then hooked hard to the face
Stoper bulled in close and the two men stood toe to to
amid the wreckage of smashed crockery and threw punche
with both hands.

Both men were big and both were powerful. Stope

weighed well over two hundred and Mahan scaled close to the one-ninety mark. Both were in excellent shape. Stoper roared in close and grabbed Marty. They went to the floor. Stabbing at Mahan's eyes with his thumbs, Stoper missed and fell forward just as Marty smashed upward with his head. Blinded by pain, Stoper was thrown off, and then Marty lunged to his feet. Stoper got up, blinking away the tears the smash had brought to his eyes. Mahan measured him with a left, then hooked right and left to the body. Yannell shook his mane of tawny hair and swung a powerful, freckled fist. It missed, and Marty hit him again in the middle. The big rider stooped and Mahan slugged him twice more and the big man wilted and went to the floor.

"Who's yellow, Yannell?" Marty said then. He mopped the sweat from his brow with a quick motion of his hand and stepped back. "Get up if you want more. You can have it."

"I'll get up!" Stoper gasped, and heaved himself erect.

Mahan stared at the swaying, punch-drunk rider. Stoper's eyes were glazed; blood dripped from his smashed lips and from a long cut over his eye. A blue mouse was rising under the other eye. His ear was bleeding. Marty stepped back and dropped his hands.

"You're no fighter," he said dryly, "an' too good a rider to beat to death!" He turned abruptly and walked out of the café.

Yannell Stoper brushed a hand dazedly across his eyes and stared after him in drunken concentration, trying to make sense of a man who would walk away from a helpless enemy. He shook his big head and, turning, staggered blindly to a chair at a vacant table. He slumped into it and rested his head on his arms.

The second day of the rodeo was a study in delay. Despite his beating of the night before, Yannell Stoper looked good. His face was raw and battered, but physically he seemed in good shape and he was fast and smooth Marty Mahan, working to absolute silence from the crowd won the finals in the calf tying by bettering his previous time by a tenth of a second. Stoper was second.

Stoper won the steer wrestling, and took the finals in the bareback bucking contest.

Marty came out on Old Seven-Seventy-Seven, a big and vicious Brahma bull who knew all the tricks. The bull weighed a shade more than a ton and had never had a stiff battle. He came out full of fight, bucking like a demon swiveling his hips, hooking left and right with his short blunted horns, fighting like mad to unseat the rider who clung to the rigging behind his hump. Marty was going and he was writing over both flanks, giving the big Brahma all the metal he could stand.

Old Seven went into a wicked spin, then suddenly reversed. The crowd gasped, expecting the speed of it to unseat Mahan, but when the dust cleared, Marty was still up there, giving the bull a spur-whipping he would never forget. The whistle blew and Mahan unloaded with a dive But Old Seven wasn't through by a whole lot. He wheeled like a cat on a hot stove and came for Marty full tilt Mahan swung around, and then the clowns dove in and one of them flicked the big bull across the nose and the maddened animal came around and went for the clown Marty walked off the tanbark to the scattered cheers of the crowd.

"Quiet today, Marty," Carver said, hesitantly.

Mahan looked up, a queer half-smile on his face. "They are waiting, Red. They want to see the Ghost Maker."

"Stoper's riding him. I lost out."

"You're lucky," Mahan said dryly. "That's no ordinary bad horse, Red. Take it from me."

Suddenly he saw Jeff Allen before him and he turned abruptly and walked toward him.

"Jeff," he said abruptly, "I want to be in the arena when Stoper rides Ghost Maker."

The older man hesitated, looking coldly at Mahan

"You had your chance to ride him," he said briefly. "Now let Stoper do it."

"I aim to," Mahan replied. "However, I don't want to see him killed!"

Allen jerked his head impatiently. "You leave that to Stoper. He ain't yellow!"

"Am I?" Marty asked quietly.

For a moment the eyes of the two men held. The hard-bitten oldster was suddenly conscious that he was wearing a gun. It was only part of the rodeo trappings, but it was loaded, and so was the gun on Mahan's hip. The days of gunfighting were past, and yet . . . Marty's eyes met his, cold and bleak.

"Why, I don't reckon you are," Jeff said suddenly. "It just seemed sort of funny, you backin' out on that horse, that's all!"

Mahan looked at him with hard eyes. "The next time something seems funny to you, Jeff, you just laugh! Hear me? Don't insinuate a man is yellow. Just laugh!" He turned on his heel and walked away.

Dick Graham looked after him thoughtfully, then said, "Jeff, I thought for a minute you were goin' to fill that long-time vacant space up in Boot Hill!"

Allen swallowed and mopped the sweat from his face. "Darned if I didn't myself!" he said, relieved. "That hombre would have drawed iron!"

"You're not just a-woofin'!" Graham said dryly. "That boy may be a lot of things, but he isn't yellow! Look what he did to Yannell last night!"

Yannell Stoper walked down to Chute Five. The Ghost Maker, a strapping big zebra dun, stood quietly waiting in the chute. He was saddled and bridled, and he made no fuss awaiting the saddle, having taken the bit calmly. Now he knew what was coming, and he waited, knowing his time was soon. Deep within his equine heart and mind something was twisted and hot, something with a slow fuse that was burning down, close to the dynamite within him.

At one side of the arena, white-faced and ready, astride his black roping horse, sat Marty Mahan. Time and again eyes strayed to him wonderingly, and one pair of those eyes belonged to Peg Graham. Yannell, despite himself, was nervous. He climbed up on the chute, waved a gloved hand, and settled in the saddle. He felt the horse bunch his muscles, then relax.

"All right," Stoper said. Then he yelled, "Cut her loose!" And then the lid blew off.

Ghost Maker left the chute with a lunge, sandwiched his head between his forelegs, and went to bucking like a horse gone mad. He was leaving the ground thirty inches at each jump and exploding with such force that blood gushed from Yannell's mouth with his third jump.

He buck-jumped wickedly in a tight circle, and then, when Yannell's head was spinning like a top, the maddened horse began to swap ends with such speed that he was almost a blur. Caught up in the insane rhythm of the pounding hoofs, Yannell was betrayed by a sudden change as the horse sprang sideways. He left the saddle and hit the ground, jarred in every vertebra.

Drunken with the pounding he had taken, he lunged to his feet, to see the horse charging him, eyes white and glaring, teeth bared. The crowd came off its seats in one long scream of horror as the maddened horse charged down on the dazed and helpless rider.

In some blind half-awareness of danger, Yannell stumbled aside. At the instant, Mahan's black horse swept down upon the maddened beast and Mahan's rope darted for the killer's head. Distracted, Ghost Maker jerked and the throw missed. Like an avenging demon he hurled himself at Marty's black, ripping a gash in the black horse's neck. The black wheeled, and the crowd screamed in horror as they saw him stumble and go down.

Out of the welter of dust and confusion somebody yelled, "Marty's up! Marty's on him!"

In the nightmare of confusion as the black fell, Marty, cold with fear of the maddened horse, grabbed out wildly and got one hand on the saddle horn of Ghost Maker. With every ounce of strength he had, he scrambled for the saddle and made it!

Out of the dust the screaming, raging horse lunged, bucking like mad, a new rider in the saddle. In some wild break of fortune, Mahan had landed with his feet in the stirrups, and now as Yannell crawled away, blood streaming from his nose, and the black threshed on the ground, Marty was up in the middle of the one horse on earth that he feared and hated.

Ghost Maker, with a bag full of tricks born in his own hate-filled brain, began to circle-buck in the same vicious tight circle that had taken Stoper from the saddle. At the height of his gyrations he suddenly began to swap ends in a blur of speed. Mahan, frightened and angry, suddenly exploded into his own private fury and began to pour steel to the horse. Across the arena they went while riders stood riveted in amazement, with Marty Mahan writing hieroglyphics all over the killer's flanks with both spurs.

Pitching like a fiend, Ghost Maker switched to straightaway bucking mingled with snakelike contortions of his spine, tightening and uncoiling like a steel spring.

Riders started cutting in from both sides, but Marty was furious now.

"Stay away!" he roared. "I'll ride him to a finish or kill him!"

And then began such a duel between horse and man as the rodeo arena at Wind River had never seen. The horse was a bundle of hate-filled energy, but the rider atop him was remembering all those long years down from his lost riding horse on the desert, and he was determined to stay with the job he had shunned. Riders circled warily out of reach, but now long after any ten-second whistle would have blown, Marty was up on the hurricane deck of the killer and whipping him to a frazzle. The horse dropped from his bucking and began to trot placidly across the arena, and then suddenly he lunged like a shot from a cannon, straight for the wall of the stands.

People screamed and sprang away as if afraid the horse might actually bound into the stands, but he wheeled and hurled his side against the board wall with force that would have crushed Marty's leg instantly. Mahan, cool and alert now, kicked his foot free and jerked the leg out of the way the instant before the horse hit.

As the animal bounded away, injured by its own mad dive, Mahan kicked his toe back into the stirrup and again began to feed steel to the tiring killer. But now the horse had had enough. Broken in spirit, he humped his back and refused to budge. For an instant Marty sat there, and then he dropped from the beaten horse to the ground and his legs almost gave way under him.

He straightened, and the killer, in one last burst of spirit, lunged at him, jaws agape. Standing his ground, Marty smashed the horse three times across the nose with his hat, and the animal backed up, thoroughly cowed.

Taking the bridle, Marty started back toward the chute, leading the beaten horse and trembling in every limb. Behind him, docile at last, walked Ghost Maker.

The emotion-wracked crowd stared at this new spectacle, and then suddenly someone started to cheer, and they were still cheering and cheering when Marty Mahan stopped by the corral and passed the bridle of the horse to a rider. He turned and leaned against the corral, still trembling. For the first time he realized that his nose was bleeding and that the front of his white rodeo costume was red with spattered blood.

Yannell Stoper, his own clothing bloody, walked up to him, hand out.

"Marty," he said sincerely, "I want to apologize. You sure ain't yella, an' you sure saved my bacon! An' that was the greatest ride a man ever made!"

"You sure weren't afraid of that horse!" Dick Graham said. "Why, man . . . !"

"Afraid of him?" Marty looked up grimly. "You're durned

right I was afraid of him! I was never so scared in my life! I didn't get on that horse because I *wanted* to! It was the safest place there was! An' once up there, I sure enough had to stay on or be killed! Scared? Mister, I was never so scared in my life!"

Old John was standing nearby grinning at him. "Nice goin', boy. An' by the way, I heard you an' the lady here"—he indicated Peg Graham—"were interested in my Willow Creek ranch outfit. If you still are, I would sell it mighty cheap, to the right couple!"

Peg was looking at him, wide-eyed and pale. "I . . . I don't know if . . . ?" Her voice was doubtful.

Marty straightened and slid an arm around her. "Sure thing, John! Looks like it would be a nice place to raise horses an' . . . "

"Cattle?" Red Carver asked, grinning.

"Kids!" Marty said. "Lots of kids! All rodeo riders!" He looked at Peg, grinning. "Okay?"

"Okay," she agreed.

The Drift

Author's Note

In the old days it was very common to see a cowboy with one or two fingers missing. Most likely there was a bad steer on the other end of the rope he had dallied around his saddle horn. His hand would get caught and a finger might get cut off or pulled off. So in every group of seven or eight cowboys you'd find one or two who had a finger gone.

Smoke Lamson came into the bunkhouse and Johnny Garrett cringed. The big foreman rolled his tobacco in his jaws and looked slowly around the room.

Nobody looked up. Nobody said anything. It was a wicked night, blowing snow and cold, so it was a foregone conclusion who was going to night-herd.

"You"—he turned suddenly to Johnny—"saddle up and get out there. An' remember, if they start to drift, make 'em circle."

Johnny swung his feet to the floor. "Why me?" he protested. "I've been on night ridin' every night this week."

Lamson grinned. "Good for you, kid. Make a man out of you. Get goin'."

An instant, Johnny Garrett hesitated. He could always quit. He could draw his time. But how long would forty dollars last? And where else could he get a job at this time of the year? Moreover, if he left the country he would never see Mary Jane again.

He drew on his boots, then his chaps and sheepskin. He pulled the rawhide under his chin and started for the door.

Lasker rolled over on his bunk. "Kid, you can take my Baldy if you want. He's a good night horse."

"Thanks," Johnny said. "I'll stick to my string. They might as well learn."

"Sure." Smoke Lamson grinned and started to build a smoke. "Like you, they gotta learn."

81

Johnny opened the door, the lamp guttered, and th
he was outside, bending his head into the wind. By n
he should be used to it.

He had come to the Bar X from Oregon, where he h
grown up in the big timber, but he came to Arizo
wanting to punch cows. After a couple of short jobs he h
stumbled into the Bar X when they needed a hand. T
boss hired him, and Lamson did not like that, but he h
said nothing, done nothing until that night in town.

Everybody on the Bar X knew that Smoke was swe
on Mary Jane Calkins. Everybody, that is, but John
Garrett. And Johnny had seen Mary Jane, danced w
her, talked with her, and then walked out with her. Loc
ing for Mary Jane, Smoke had found them in a swi
together.

He had been coldly furious, and Mary Jane, appare
unaware of what she was doing, told Smoke that John
was going to be a top hand by spring. "You wait an' se
Johnny had said.

And Smoke Lamson looked at Johnny and grinn
slowly. "You know, Mary Jane," he said meaningfully, "
bet he is!"

That started it. Every tough and lonely job fell
Johnny Garrett. Morning, noon, and night he was on ca
Everybody in the bunkhouse could see that Smoke w
riding Johnny, driving him, trying to make him qu
"Want to be a top hand, don't you?" he would taunt. "C
on out there!" And Johnny went.

He mended what seemed to be miles of fence, and
Lamson did not think it was well done, it was done ov
He cut wood for the cook, the lowest of cow ranch jobs;
hunted strays in the wildest and roughest country; he us
a shovel more than a rope, cleaning water-holes, openi
springs. He did more night riding than any three men
the outfit. He worked twelve and fourteen hours a d

when the others rarely did more than seven or eight in the fall and bitter winter.

Smoke Lamson was big and he was tough. It was his boast that he had never been bested in a rough-and-tumble fight, and although he outweighed Johnny by forty pounds, he seemed to be trying to tempt the smaller man to try his luck.

As the months went by it grew worse. As if angered by his failure to force Johnny to quit, Lamson became tougher. Even Lasker, a taciturn man, attempted to reason with Smoke. "Why don't you lay off the kid?" he demanded. "He's doin' his job."

"My business, Dan." Smoke was abrupt. "When he's as good a hand as you or me, I'll lay off."

Johnny got the saddle on his dun and rode out of the big barn, ducking his head under the door. From the saddle he swung the door shut, then turned the horse into the wind and headed toward the west range.

Ice was already forming and the ground had white patches of snow, but there was more in the air, blowing as well as falling, than on the ground. It was blowing cold and bitter from the north, and if the cattle started to drift and got any kind of a start, there would be no stopping them. Not far below the valley where he would be riding was Sage Flat, fifty miles wide and half again that long, and nothing to stop them in all that length but a forty-foot arroyo. If they started south ahead of the wind, they would be half-frozen by the time they reached that arroyo and would walk off into it.

Johnny had heard about a drift. He had never seen it, but his imagination was good.

He had been in the saddle over an hour when he saw the first steer, a big roan steer, heading toward him, plodding steadily. Behind him there was another, then another . . . and for the first time, he knew panic.

Deep inside he knew that nobody had ever expected this. The upper end of the valley he patrolled was fenced, and Smoke had sent him here just for safety's sake or out of pure cussedness, but the fence must be down, must have been pushed over, and they were coming.

There was no time to go for help. He drew his pistol and fired into the air, partly hoping to stop the drift, partly to call for help. It did neither. Desperately, he tried to turn the cattle, and they would not turn. When he got one half-turned into the storm, others would go by him.

And from up the valley came more, and more, and more.

Then he realized the full enormity of what was happening. The whole herd, more than a thousand head, would be drifting ahead of the norther. Unless stopped they would drift into the arroyo, winding up at the bottom either dead or with broken legs, helpless, for the cold to kill. A few would survive, of course, but not many. A forty-foot fall into a rocky ravine is not calculated to do either man or animal any good.

The dun worked hard. Johnny yelled, fired more shots, tried everything. The cattle kept coming. He had forgotten Smoke Lamson, who had sent him here. He had forgotten everything but the cattle and the kindly old man, old Bart Gavin, who had hired him when he was broke.

He drew up, staring into the storm. Ice was forming on the scarf over his chin. His toes were numb from inactivity, and the cattle drifted. It was four miles to the gate, four more to the bunkhouse. To go there and get back with the hands—for they must all dress and saddle up—would let too many cattle go by. And what could be done when they got here?

By daybreak a thousand head of beef steers would be piled up along a mile or so of that arroyo. Unless . . . unless he could force them over. If he could push them east to the flank of Comb Ridge, start them down along the ridge until they got between the ridge and Gavin

Fault, he might force them to pile up in one place. Some would be lost but the fall of the others would be cushioned. . . . An idea clicked in his mind.

Swinging the startled dun, he slammed the spurs to the mustang and raced south. He passed steer after steer, plodding steadily, methodically on, hypnotized by their movement and driven by the howling norther behind them. Racing on at breakneck speed over the frozen ground, he was soon beyond them. As he raced, he was thinking. They were traveling slow, the usual slow walk of a drift herd. There would be, with luck, time enough.

Soon he was passing the straggling leaders, strung out for a quarter of a mile, and then he was racing alone into the night and the south, away from the herd, toward the arroyo. Yet, when a few miles were behind him he swung off west and rode hard. Suddenly he saw a shoulder of Gavin Fault, a huge upthrust of sandstone. Keeping it close on his left, he rode down it until against the night he caught the square shoulder of Rock House. He swung the dun into the lee of the house and got out of the saddle.

The door opened when he lifted the latch and shoved. He got in quickly and struck a match. Against the wall were piled four boxes of powder. He stuffed it into sacks, caught up a roll of fuse, and ran from the shack, closing the door after him.

Putting the giant powder behind the saddle, he got up himself, and, the fuses around his arm, heedless of risk, he rode on south. If the dun stumbled and fell—well, there would be a mighty big hole in the grass!

The dun liked to run, and it was bitter cold now. How cold he did not know, but getting down there. He raced onward until suddenly he saw ahead of him the black line of the arroyo. He swung from the dun and led the horse into the shelter of a rocky projection and hurried to the edge. Carefully, he clambered down.

He knew that spot. He had slipped away and hidden from Lamson to catch a quiet smoke on several occasions. It was cracked and honeycombed with holes. Working swiftly, he stuffed the cracks with powder, jammed bunches of sticks into holes, and worked his way from the lip almost to the bottom. He had been working for more than a half hour before he saw the first steer. It had brought up against a rock some distance off and stood there, befuddled. It would soon come on.

Sheltered from the wind that blew over the lip above him, Johnny ran along, hastily spitting his fuses. When all were lighted that he could see, he scrambled back up and grabbed his horse. He was riding into the teeth of the wind when he heard the blast. There was no time to go back. It had to work. It must work.

North he rode until he saw the cattle. They were coming now in droves, and soon he was past the end of the fault. Channeled by the valley from which they had come, the animals plodded steadily ahead. Only a few seemed inclined to stray west, and these he pushed back. He could move them east or west, but no power on earth could now prevent them from going south.

How long he worked he did not know. Every move might be futile. Once the dun fell, but scrambled gamely up. Soon Johnny found a place from which he could watch for some distance. The snow was letting up, the ground was white, and visibility not bad. He worked more slowly, half-dead in the saddle, and then the last of the cattle drifted by and he turned his horse and walked slowly back to the ranch.

Half-dead with weariness, he stripped the saddle from his horse and then went to work. For half an hour he worked hard over the dun, and then he blanketed the horse to allow him to conserve as much heat as possible. Stumbling, he got into the bunkhouse and crawled into bed. His feet were numbed and for a while he held his toes, trying to warm them. And then he fell asleep.

A hand on his shoulder awakened him. It was Dan Lasker. "Better crawl out, kid. Lamson's on a tear this mornin'."

He was the last one to reach the breakfast table. He

came into the room and stopped abruptly. Sitting with
Bart Gavin was a girl . . . and what a girl!

Her hair was dark and thick, her eyes bright, her lips
slightly full and red. In a daze he got into a chair and
hitched close to the table. The hands were tongue-tied.
No conversation this morning. In front of the radiant
creature beside Bart they were completely at a loss. Even
Smoke Lamson was speechless.

Suddenly, she spoke. "Why is it that only one of the
horses has a blanket on him? It was so cold last night!"

"Blanket?" Gavin looked around. "Blanket on a horse?"

The hands looked around, astonished. The tough Western cow ponies were unaccustomed to such treatment.
Even Smoke Lamson was surprised. Suddenly he turned
on Johnny, seeing a chance to have some fun. "Maybe it
was the Top Hand here. That sounds like him."

The dark and lovely eyes turned to Johnny and he
blushed furiously.

"Did oo w'ap up the po' itto hossie?" Lamson said,
glancing at the girl to see if his wit was appreciated, and
chuckling.

Gavin looked at Johnny sharply. Feeling some explanation necessary, Johnny said feebly, "He was pretty wore
out. It was near to daybreak before I got in."

Gavin put his fork down. "Daybreak?" He was incredulous. "What were you doing out last night?"

It was Lamson's turn to grow confused. He hesitated.
Then he said, "I figured somebody better watch in case of
a drift."

"A *drift*?" Gavin's voice was scornful. "With that fence?
It's horse high and bull strong! Anyway"—his voice was
biting—"what could one man do against a drift?"

Smoke Lamson stuttered, hesitated, and finally tried a
feeble excuse. The girl looked from him to Johnny, and
then at the other hands. Bart Gavin was no fool. He was
beginning to realize something he had not realized before.

"The cows are all right." Johnny found a voice. "I was
there when the drift started. They are in the arroyo."

"*What?*" Bart Gavin came out of his seat, his face shocked and pale.

All eyes were on Johnny now. "I never did figure out what happened to the fence. I was ridin', then all of a sudden I seem 'em comin'. I shot off my gun an' yelled, but nobody heard me, an' it didn't have any effect on the cows."

Lamson was hoarse. "You mean . . . there was a drift? They got through the fence?"

"Yeah," Johnny said, "but they are all right."

"What do you mean"—Gavin's voice was icy—"all right? You mean I've got forty thousand dollars' worth of cattle piled up in the arroyo?"

"They ain't piled," Johnny explained. "Not many, at least. I seen—saw—what was goin' to happen, so I got that powder out of the Rock House and blowed—I mean, I blew the edge of the arroyo. I figure they couldn't go no further, so they are probably scattered up an' down it."

There was a long moment of deathly silence. Lamson was pale, the others incredulous. Gavin stared at Johnny, and after a minute he picked up his fork and started to eat. "Let me get this straight," he said. "You got ahead of the heard, blew off the edge of the arroyo, then got back and worked all night pointing those cattle toward the break?"

"It wasn't much." Johnny was sheepish. "I had 'em narrowed down by the valley, so I just had to keep 'em that way."

"I think that was wonderful!" the girl with the dark eyes said. "Don't you, Uncle Bart?"

"It saved me the best part of forty thousand dollars, is all." Gavin was emphatic. "Lamson, I want to talk to you. First, we'll take a look."

Of the more than a thousand cattle that drifted south, only six were lost. Despite the hurry and the darkness, Johnny had chosen his spot well and the powder had been well planted. Knowing the arroyo, he had known how many cracks were in the rocky edge, and how honeycombed it was with holes eroded by wind and water.

Gavin found his cattle scattered along the bottom of he arroyo, feeding on the rich grass that grew there vhere water often stood. He studied the blasted edge, ;lancing sharply at Johnny. "You knew something about 1owder, son," he said. "Those shots were well placed."

"My dad had a claim up in Oregon," Johnny explained. I helped him some, doin' assignment work."

What Bart Gavin said to Lamson none of them knew, 1ut for a few days his driving of Johnny ceased, although ome sneering remarks about "pets" were made. And then ;radually the old way resumed. It was Johnny Garrett who Irew the rough jobs.

When there was to be a dance at Rock Springs School-1ouse, where Johnny might have seen Mary Jane, he was ent to a line-camp at Eagle Rest.

It was a rugged, broken country, heavily timbered like 1is native Oregon, but riven by canyons and peaks, and ut here and there by lava flows and bordered on the east 1y the *malpais*, a forty-mile-wide stretch of lava where no 1orse could go and where a man's boots would be cut to ibbons in no time. Supposedly waterless, it was a treach-rous area. There were stretches of flat, smooth lava, 1nnocent in appearance, but actually that seemingly solid ock was merely the thin dome over a lava blister. Step-1ing on it, a man could plunge fifteen to fifty feet into a avernous hole whose sides were slick and impossible to limb.

The few openings into this *malpais* were fenced, and 1e fences had to be kept up. At places the lava rode in a vall of basaltic blocks.

After the water holes were cleaned, salt scattered, and 1e fences checked, there was little to do. Johnny had a :olt and a Winchester, and he did a lot of shooting. He :illed two mountain lions and a half-dozen wolves, skin-1ing them and tanning the hides.

A week later Lasker rode in with two pack horses of

supplies. Lasker was a tall, rawboned man who had punche
cows for fifteen years.

He noticed the hides but made no comment. Hun
kered down by the wall in the morning sun, he said, "Ol
man's worried. The tally fell off this year. He's losin
cows."

"You seen Mary Jane?"

"She was at the dance with Smoke," Lasker said, starte
to say something further, but stopped. Then he said
" 'Member that niece of Gavin's? She's livin' at the ranch
Her name is Betty."

"Too high-toned for any cowpunch."

"Can't tell about a woman," Lasker said. "Some of th
high-toned ones are thoroughbreds."

Two days later Johnny found a dead cow. Wolves ha
torn it, but the cow had been shot in the head . . . th
carcass not even a week old. Nobody had been around bu
Lasker and himself.

It was a Gavin cow. The only reason to shoot a cow wa
because she followed a rustled calf. Johnny was woods
bred and he spelled out the trail. A dozen head of youn
stuff had been taken through the timber into high country
He followed the scuffed trail through the pine needles
then lost it at the rim of a high canyon about the *malpais*

For a week he scouted for sign, keeping up the pre
tense of only doing his work. Once, he cut the trail of
shod horse but lost it. Back at the cabin he began t
sketch a crude map on brown wrapping paper, incorporat
ing all he knew of the country, marking ridges, arroyos
and streams.

Three small streams disappeared in the direction of th
lava beds, and nobody had ever followed those streams t
see where they went. Both streams were shallow—n
water backed up anywhere.

The first stream, he discovered, veered suddenly sout
and dropped from sight in a deep cavern under the lava

Two days later, mending fence, he checked the next stream. It ended in a swamp.

Lasker and Lamson rode in the following day. Lasker was friendly and noticed the fresh wolf hide. "Good huntin'?"

"Yeah, but not enough time."

Smoke Lamson said nothing, but looked around carefully, and several times Johnny found Smoke watching him intently. It was not until they were about to leave that Lamson turned suddenly. "Seen anybody? Any strange riders?"

"Not a soul," Johnny told him, and after they were gone he swore at himself for not mentioning the tracks. And the cow.

On the third day after that, he circled around to trace the source of the one unexplored stream. When he found it he rode into the water and had followed it downstream more than a mile when he heard voices. He could distinguish no words, but two men were talking. Through a veil of brush he saw them ride out of the trees. One was a fat, sloppy man in a dirty gray shirt. The other was lean and savage; his name was Hoyt, and Johnny had seen him in town. He was said to be dangerous. After they were gone, Johnny followed cautiously.

The stream's current increased. It was dropping fast, and suddenly he found himself about to enter a sheer-walled canyon. Climbing his dun out of the water, he followed along the rim for more than an hour as the canyon grew deeper, until the riders were mere dots.

In a clearing atop the mountain, Johnny took his bearings. To north, south, and east lay the *malpais*, spotted with trees and brush that concealed the razorlike edges of broken lava. Suppose there was, far out there where the stream flowed, a grassy valley where stolen cattle were held?

Back at the cabin he made his decision. It was time to

talk to Bart Gavin. Switching horses he rode back, arriving long after dark. It would take another day to return, but he must see the rancher. "Nobody home," the cook told him. "All gone to dance. Only Dan, he here."

Lasker sat up when Johnny walked into the bunkhouse. "Hey, what's up?" The sleep was gone from his eyes.

"Needed tobacco," Johnny lied glibly. He sat down. "A dance in town?"

Lasker relaxed. "So that's it? Kid, you'll get Lamson sore. You shouldn't oughta have come in."

"Aw, why not? Climb into your duds an' we'll ride. I want to see Mary Jane."

Riding into the outskirts, Lasker said, "That's a staked claim, kid. Better lay off." Then he added, "He's a fighter."

"So'm I. I grew up in lumber camps."

As they tied their horses, Lasker said again, "Stay away from Mary Jane. She ain't for you, kid, an'—"

Johnny turned to face him. "What's wrong with her?"

Lasker started to speak, then shrugged. "Your funeral."

Mary Jane squealed excitedly when she saw him. "Why Johnny! I thought you were 'way up in the woods. What brought you back?"

"I had a reason." He liked being mysterious. "You'll know soon enough."

During the second dance she kept insisting. "What reason, Johnny? Why did you come back?"

"Secret," he said. "You'll know before long."

"Tell me. I won't tell anybody."

"It's nothing." He shrugged it off. "Only I found some rustlers."

"You *found* them?" Her eyes were bright. "Why John—!"

A big hand fell on his shoulder and he was spun into a hard fist crashing out of nowhere. He started to fall, but the second blow caught and knocked him sprawling.

Johnny's head was buzzing but he rolled over and got up swiftly. Smoke Lamson, his face hard and angry, swung wickedly, and Johnny clinched. Lamson hurled him to the floor, and before Johnny could scramble to his feet, Smoke rushed in and swung his leg for a kick. Johnny threw himself at Lamson's legs and they hit the floor in a heap. Coming up fast they walked into each other, punching with both hands. Johnny had the shorter reach but he got inside. He slammed a right to the ribs and Lamson took an involuntary step back. Then Johnny smashed a left to his face and, crouching, hooked a right to the body.

Around them the crowd was yelling and screaming. In the crowd was Mary Jane, her face excited, and nearby another face. That of the fat, sloppy man from the canyon!

Lamson rushed, but, over his momentary shock from the unexpected punch, Johnny was feeling good. Due to the brutally hard labor of the preceding fall and winter he was in fine shape. He was lithe as a panther and rugged as a Texas steer. He ducked suddenly and tackled Lamson. The big man fell hard and got up slowly. Johnny knocked him down. Lamson got up and Johnny threw him with a rolling hip-lock, and when the bigger man tried to get up again, Johnny knocked him down again.

His face bloody, Lamson stayed down. "Awright, kid. You whupped me."

Johnny backed off and then walked away. Mary Jane was nowhere in sight. Disappointed, he looked around again. Across the room he saw Gavin and his niece. Betty was looking at him, and she was smiling. He started toward them when something nudged his ribs and a cool voice said, "All right, kid, let's go outside an' talk."

"But I—"

"Right now. An' don't get any fancy ideas. You wouldn't be the first man I killed." The man with the gun in his back was Hoyt, the gun held so it could not be seen. They walked from the hall, and Betty looked after them, bewildered.

The fat rustler was waiting. He had Johnny's horse and theirs. Johnny moved toward his horse, remembering the pistol he had thrust into the saddlebag and the rifle in the scabbard. He reached for the pommel and a gun barrel came down over his skull. He started to fall, caught a second glancing blow, and dropped into a swirling darkness.

The lurching of the horse over the stones of the creek brought him to consciousness. The feel under his leg told him the rifle was gone. His ankles were tied, and his wrists. Was the pistol still in the saddlebag?

Pain racked his skull, and some time later he passed out again, coming out of it only when they took him off his horse and shoved him against the cabin wall. He was in a long grassy valley, ringed with *malpais*, but a valley of thousands of acres.

A third man came from the cabin. Johnny remembered him as cook for one of the roundup outfits, named Freck. "Grub's on," Freck said, nodding briefly at Johnny.

They ate in silence. Hoyt watched Johnny without making a point of it. Freck and the fat man ate noisily. "You tell anybody about this place?" Hoyt demanded.

"Maybe," Johnny said. "I might have."

"Horse comin'," Hoyt said suddenly. "See who it is, Calkins."

Johnny stiffened. Calkins . . . Mary Jane's father. Something died within him. He stared at his food, appetite gone. It had been Mary Jane, then, who told the rustlers he had found the cattle and the hideout. No wonder she had been curious. No wonder they had rushed him out before he could talk to Gavin.

Calkins stood in the door with a Winchester. Turning his head, he said, "It's the boss."

A hard, familiar voice called, then footsteps. Johnny saw Dan Lasker step into the door. Lasker's smile was bleak. "Hello, Johnny. It ain't good to see you."

"Never figured you for a rustler."

"Man can't get rich at forty a month, Johnny." He squatted on his heels against the wall. "We need another man." Lasker lit a smoke. He seemed worried. "You're here, kid."

It was a way out and there would be no other. And

asker wanted him to take it. Actually speaking, there was
o choice.

"Are you jokin'?" Johnny's voice was sarcastic. "Only
ing I can't figure is why you didn't let me in on it from
ie start." And he lied quietly: "I was figurin' to moon-
ght a few cows myself, only I couldn't find a way out of
ie country."

Lasker was pleased. "Good boy, Johnny. As for a way
ut, we've got it."

Hoyt shoved back from the table. "All I can say is, one
rong move outa this kid, an' I'll handle it my own way!"

"All right, Hoyt." Lasker measured him coolly. "But
e double-damned sure you're right."

They had over four hundred stolen cattle and were
eady for a drive. But they did not return Johnny's guns.
or did he make as much as a move toward his saddlebags.

Calkins came in midway of the following afternoon. He
as puffing and excited. "Rider comin'. An' it's that young
iece of Gavin's!"

Hoyt got up swiftly. "Dan, I don't like it!"

Freck walked to the door and waited there, watching
er come. "What difference does it make? She's here, an'
ie ain't goin' back. Nobody ever found this place, and it's
ot likely they have now."

"What I want to know," Hoyt said bitterly, "is how she
und it."

"Probably followed the kid." Lasker was uneasy and
owed it. "She's sweet on him."

Betty Gavin was riding a black mare and she cantered
p, smiling. "Hello, Johnny! Hello, Dan! Gee, I'm glad I
und you! I thought I was lost."

"How'd you happen to get here?" Lasker inquired. He
as puzzled. She seemed entirely unaware that anything
as wrong. But being an eastern girl, how could she
ow? On the other hand, how could an eastern girl have
ot here?

"Uncle Bart was at the old place on Pocketpoint, so decided I'd ride over and surprise Johnny. I lost my wa and then I saw some horse tracks, so I followed then When I got in that canyon I was scared, but there was way to get out, so I kept coming."

She looked around. "So this is what Eagle's Nest like?"

Johnny Garrett was appalled. Calkins was frownin Hoyt was frankly puzzled, as was Lasker. Yet Lasker looke relieved. He was not a murderer nor a man who wou harm a woman, and this offered a way out. If Betty did n know the difference—

She came right up to Johnny, smiling. "My, but you' a mess!" she said. "Straighten your handkerchief." Sh reached up and pulled it around and he felt somethir sharp against the skin of his neck under the collar. It was fold of paper. "Are you going to take me back to Pocketpoint

"Can't," he said. "But maybe Dan will. I'm busy here

He scratched his neck, palmed the paper, and when opportunity offered, he got a glimpse of it. The paper w the brown wrapping paper upon which he had worked o his first map of the streams and the probable route in this valley, with his notes.

She had lied then. She had come from Eagle's Ne following his own map, and she knew exactly where sh was! He looked at her in astonishment. How could she b so cool? So utterly innocent?

He began to roll a smoke, thinking this out. Lask might take her out of here. He could be trusted with woman, and the others could not. Out of the corners of h eyes, he measured the distance to the saddlebag. N good. They'd kill him before he got it open. Unless . . He hesitated. Unless he was very careful about it—

Lasker, Calkins, and Hoyt had moved off to one sic and were talking. Betty glanced at Johnny. "I was afraid wouldn't find you," she said, low-voiced.

Freck could hear them, but there were two meanings here.

"Won't Bart be worried?"

"Yes, he probably will. I"—she looked right at him—"left a note at the cabin." *A note at the line cabin!* Then there was a chance!

Suddenly, Freck was speaking. "Hoyt," he said, "we better look at our hole card. That gal's got red mud on her boot. Ain't no place got red mud but around the cabin at Eagle's Nest."

Johnny felt his mouth go dry. He saw Betty's face change color, and he said quietly, "You don't know what you're sayin', Freck. There's red mud behind the cabin at Pocketpoint."

Hoyt looked at Calkins. "Is there? You been there?"

"I been there. Dogged if I can recall!"

Hoyt's eyes were suddenly hard. He turned a little so his lank body was toward Lasker. Almost instinctively, Calkins drew back, but Freck's loyalty to Hoyt was obvious.

"Got a present for you, Betty." Johnny spoke into the sudden silence. His voice seemed unusually loud. "Aimed to bring it down first chance I got. One of those agates I was tellin' you about."

He walked to his saddlebag, and behind him he heard Hoyt say, "We can't let that girl leave here, Dan."

"Don't be a fool!" Lasker's anger was plain. "You can steal cattle and get away with it. Harm a girl like this and the West isn't big enough to hide us!"

"I'll gamble. But if she goes out, we're finished. Our work done for nothin'."

"Keep her," Freck said. "She'd be company." He winked at Lasker.

All eyes were watching Hoyt. It was there the trouble would start. Johnny ran his hand down into the saddlebag and came up with the .44 Colt. He turned, the gun concealed by his body.

"She goes," Lasker said, "cattle or no cattle."

"Over my dead body!" Hoyt snapped, and his hand dropped for his gun.

Freck grabbed iron, too, and Johnny yelled. The cook swung his head and Johnny's pistol came up. Johnny shot and swung his gun. Calkins backed away, hands high and his head shaking.

Guns were barking, and Johnny turned. Lasker was down and Hoyt was weaving on his feet. Hoyt stared at Lasker. "We had him, Freck an' me, just like we figured! Had him boxed, in a cross-fire! Then you—!" His gun came up and Johnny fired, then fired again. Hoyt went down and rolled over.

Johnny wheeled on Calkins. "Drop your belt!" His voice was hard. "Now get in there an' get some hot water!"

He moved swiftly to Betty. "Are you all right?"

Her face was pale, her eyes wide and shocked. "All right," she whispered. "I'll be all right."

Johnny ran to Lasker. The cowhand lay sprawled on the ground and he had been shot twice. Once through the chest, once through the side. But he was still alive. . . .

Bart Gavin and four hands rode in an hour later. Gavin stopped abruptly when he saw the bodies, then came on in. Betty ran to him.

Johnny came to the door. "Me an' Dan," he said, "we had us a run-in with some rustlers. In the shootout Dan was wounded. With luck, he'll make it."

Bart Gavin had one arm around his niece. "Betty saw Hoyt take you out, but we thought she was imagining things, so when she couldn't make us believe, she took off on her own. Naturally, we trailed her . . . and found her note and your map, traced out."

Gavin saw Calkins. His face grew stern. "What's he doin' here?"

Johnny said quietly, "He stayed out of it. He was

ustlin', but when it came to Betty, he stayed out. I told
im we'd let him go."

Inside the cabin they stood over Lasker. He was con-
cious, and he looked up at them. "That was white, mighty
hite of you."

"Need you," Johnny said quietly. "Gavin just told me
e fired Lamson. He said he'd been watchin' my work, an'
m the new foreman. You're workin' for me now."

"For us," Betty said. "As long as he wants."

Lasker grinned faintly. "Remember what I said, kid?
hat some of the high-toned gals were thoroughbreds?"

No Rest
for the Wicked

■———————————■———————————■

Author's Note

It takes two kinds of men to develop a mining country: the men who find the mines and the men who develop them, and they are rarely the same person. The prospector, the discoverer, is not often equipped in money and the business ability to open up and develop a mine. Many of them sold their claim off for what seemed nothing. And yet it was to them a great deal. And if they'd persisted in opering their mines they might have lost everything.

Some men only wanted what they could take out by themselves. They kept their discoveries a secret, going back again and again to take out what they needed, and when they died—of disease, accident, or gun play—the mine's location was lost.

From the ridge on my Colorado ranch I can look across a bunch of mountains where there are dozens of lost mines. At least two of them are somewhere in the range of my vision. Find them? It isn't easy. It's a big, big country and prospecting is a slow, painstaking operation. Since prospectors gave up the burro for the Jeep, fewer mines are found. Jeeps can't go into the roughest country, and many of the best mines were found at places where no man in his right mind would want to go.

The bat-wing doors slammed open as if struck by a charging steer and he stood there, framed for an instant in the doorway, a huge man with a golden beard and magnificent shoulders.

Towering five inches over six feet and weighing no less than two hundred and fifty pounds, he appeared from out of the desert like some suddenly reincarnated primeval giant.

He was dirty, not with the dirt of indigence, but with the dust and grime of travel. He smelled of the trail, and his cheekbones had a desert bronze upon them. As he strode to the bar there was something reckless and arrogant about him that raised the hackles on the back of my neck.

Stopping near me he called for a bottle, and when he had it in his hand he poured three fingers into a water glass and took it neat. He followed with its twin before he paused to look around.

He glanced at the tables where men played cards, and then at the roulette wheel. His eyes rested on the faces of the gamblers, and then at last, they swung around to me. Oh, I knew he was coming to me! He had seen me when he came in, but he saved me for last.

His look measured me and assayed me with a long, deliberately contemptuous glance. For I am a big man, too, and the difference between us was slight.

Yet where he was golden, I was black, and where the heat had reddened his cheekbones, I was deep-browned by sun and wind. We measured each other like two strange mastiffs, and neither of us liked the other.

He looked from my eyes to the star on my chest, and to the gun low-slung on my leg. He grinned then, a slow insulting grin. "The town clown," he said.

"Exactly," I replied, and smiled at him. For I could see it then, knew it was coming, and I could afford to wait. He measured me again when he saw that I did not anger.

He changed suddenly, shrugging, and smiled. "No offense," he said, and his smile seemed genuine. "I've got a loose tongue." He reached in his pocket and drew out three pieces of ore and rolled them on the bar. "Besides, feel too good to make trouble for anybody today. I've found the Lost Village Diggings."

His voice had not lifted a note, and yet had he shouted the words he could have received no more attention. Every head turned; men came to their feet; all eyes were on him, all ears listening.

"*The Lost Village Diggings!*" Old Tom Curtis grabbed the stranger by the arm. "You've found 'em? You actually have? Where?"

The big man chuckled. "Didn't aim to get you folks upset," he said. "Look for yourself." He nudged the ore with his fist. "How's that look?"

Curtis grabbed up the ore. His eyes were hot with excitement. He was almost moaning in his reverence. "Why! Why, it must run three or four thousand dollars to the ton! *Look* at it!"

The chunks of ore were ribbed with gold, bright and lovely to see, but I spared the gold only a glance. My eyes were on the stranger, and I was waiting.

They crowded around him, shouting their questions, eager to see and to handle the ore. He poured another drink, looked at me, then grinned. He lifted the glass in a silent toast.

Yet I think it bothered him. The rest of them were crazy with gold fever, but I was not. And he didn't understand it.

The Lost Village Diggings! Stories of lost mines crop up wherever one goes in the Southwest, but this one was even more fantastic than most. In 1609 three Franciscan friars, accompanied by an officer and sixteen soldiers, started north out of Mexico.

Attacked by Apaches, they turned back, and finally were surrounded among rough mountains by the Indians. During the night they attempted to escape and became lost. By daylight they found themselves moving through utterly strange country, and their directions seemed all wrong. All of them felt curiously confused.

Yet they had escaped the Indians. Thankfully, they kept on, getting deeper and deeper into unfamiliar country. On the third day they found themselves in a long canyon through which wound a stream of fresh, clear water. There were wide green meadows, rich soil, and a scattering of trees. Weary of their flight, they gratefully settled down for a rest. And then they found gold.

The result was, instead of going on, they built houses and a church, and remained to mine the rich ore and reduce it to raw gold. Accompanied by one of the Indians who had come with them, for there had been a dozen of these, four soldiers attempted to find a way out to Mexico. All were killed but one, who returned. Attracted by the healing of one of the Franciscans, several Tarahumares came to live among them, and then more. Several of the soldiers took wives from the Indian girls and settled down. Lost to the outside world, the village grew, cultivated fields, and was fairly prosperous. And they continued to mine gold.

Yet a second attempt to get out of the valley also failed, with three men killed. It was only after thirty years had passed that an Indian succeeded. He got through to Mexico and reported the village. Guiding the party on the return trip, he was bitten by a snake and died.

In 1750 two wandering Spanish travelers stumbled upon a faint trail and followed it to the village. It had grown to a tight, neatly arranged settlement of more than one hundred inhabitants. The travelers left, taking several villagers with them, but they likewise were killed by Apaches. Only one man got through, adding his story to the legend of the Lost Village. From that day on it was never heard of again.

"All my life," Old Tom Curtis said, "I've hoped I'd find that Village! Millions! Millions in gold there, all stored and waiting to be took! A rich mine! Maybe several of 'em!"

The big man with the golden beard straightened up. "My name's Larik Feist," he said. "I found the Lost Village by accident. I was back in the Sierra Madres, and wounded a boar. I chased after him, got lost, and just stumbled on her."

"Folks still there?" Curtis asked eagerly.

"Nobody," Feist said. "Not a soul. Dead for years looks like." He leaned against the bar and added three fingers to his glass. "But I found the mine—two of 'em! found their *arrastra*, too!"

"But the gold?" That was Bob Wright, owner of the livery stable. "Did you find the gold?"

"Not yet," Feist admitted, "but she's got to be there."

There was an excited buzz of talk, but I turned away and leaned against the bar. There was nothing I could say and nobody who would believe me. I knew men with the gold fever; I'd seen others have it. So I waited, knowing what was coming, and thinking about Larik Feist.

"Sure," Feist said, "I'm goin' back. Think I'm crazy? Apaches? Never seen a one, but what if I did? No Apache will keep me away from there. But I got to get an outfit."

"I'll stake you," Wright said quickly. "I'll furnish the horses and mules."

Men crowded around, tendering supplies, equipment, guns, experience. Feist didn't accept; he just shook his head. "First thing I need," he said, "is some rest. I won't even think about it until morning."

He straightened up and gathered his samples. Reluctantly, the others drew back. Feist looked over at me. "What's the matter, Marshal?" he taunted. "No gold fever?"

"Once," I said, "I had it."

"He sure did!" Old Tom Curtis chuckled. "Why, he was only a boy, but he sure spent some time down there. Say! He'd be a good man to take along! The marshal sure knows the Sierra Madres!"

Feist had started to move away. Now he stopped. His face had a queer look. "You've been there?" he demanded.

"Yes." I spoke quietly. "I've been there."

That was the beginning of it. Larik Feist avoided me, but his plans went forward rapidly. A company was formed with Feist as president, Wright as treasurer, and Dave Neil as vice-president. When I heard that, I walked down to Neil's house. Marla was out in the yard, picking flowers.

"Your dad home?"

She straightened and nodded to me. It seemed she was absent-minded—not like she usually was when I came around. I stood there, and I looked myself over in her eyes. I was a big man, two inches shorter than Feist, and maybe twenty pounds less in weight. Yet I'm mighty spare and muscular, and folks generally figure me to weigh no more than two hundred and a few pounds.

So I knew what she saw, a big man with wide, thick shoulders and a chest that stretched in his shirt tight. With a brown, wind-darkened face and green eyes, a shock of black, curly, and unusually untrimmed hair, a battered black sombrero, flat crowned, a faded checked shirt, jeans, and boots with run-down heels. And two big guns that looked small on me.

Feist was different. He had the trail dust off him now and a new outfit of clothes, bought on credit. He looked slick and handsome; his hair was trimmed. He was the talk of the town, with all the girls making big eyes at him. They all knew me. They all knew Lou Morgan, who was half-Irish and half-Spanish.

"Yes, Dad's inside talking to Larik," she said. "Isn't he wonderful?"

That hurt, Marla? Well, I'd always figured on Marla being my girl. We'd gone dancing together, we'd been riding together, and we'd talked some about the future—when I'd made my stake and owned a ranch.

"Wonderful?" I shook my head. "That doesn't seem like the right word."

"Oh, Lou!" She was impatient. "Don't be like that! Here Larik comes to town and offers us all a chance to be rich, and you stand around—they all told me how you acted—just like . . . like . . . like you were jealous of him!"

"Why should I be jealous?" I asked.

Her eyes chilled a little. "Oh? You don't think I'm worth being jealous over?"

That made me look at her again. "Oh! So you're in this, too? It's not only all the town's money he wants, but you, too."

"You've no right to talk that way! I like Larik! He's wonderful! And he's doing something for us all!"

Right then I couldn't trust myself to talk. I just walked by her and went into the house. Neil was there, seated at the table with Feist, Wright, Curtis, and John Powers. They all had money on the table, and some sort of legal looking papers.

"What's the money for?" I asked, quiet-like.

"We're buyin' into Mr. Feist's mine," Powers said. "You'd better dig down in that sock of yours and get a piece of this, Lou. We'll need a good man to protect that gold." Powers turned to Feist and jerked a head at me. "Lou, here, is about the fastest thing with a gun this side of Dodge."

Feist looked up at me, his eyes suddenly cold and careful.

Me, I didn't look at him. "Neil," I said, "do you mean to tell me you men are all paying good cash for something you've never seen? That you're buyin' a pig in a poke?"

"Never seen?" Neil said. "What does that matter?

e've seen the gold, haven't we? We all know the Lost
illage story, and—"

"All you know," I said, "is an old legend that's been
ld around for years. You're all like a pack of kids taken in
y a slick-talking stranger. Feist"—I looked across the
ble at him—"you're under arrest. Obtaining money un-
er false pretenses."

Neil lunged to his feet. His face was flushed with
nger. "Lou, what's the matter? Have you gone crazy?"

All of them were on their feet protesting. Only Larik
eist had not moved, but for the first time he looked
orried.

It was Marla who made it worse. "Dad," she said, "pay
o attention to him. Lou's jealous. He's made big tracks
round here so long he can't stand for anybody to take the
imelight."

That made me red around the gills because it was so
ntrue. "You think what you like, but I'm taking Feist
ow."

Feist looked at me, a long measuring look from those
old, careful eyes. He had it in his mind.

"Don't go for that gun," I said quietly. "I want you
ried in a court of law, not dead on this floor."

Powers put a hand on Feist's arm. "Go along with
im," he said. "And don't worry. We'll take care of you.
'ar as that goes, we can call a meeting and throw him out
f office."

"I'm arresting Feist," I said patiently. "You do what-
ver you want."

"On what evidence?" Neil demanded.

"I'll present the evidence when it's needed," I said.
Take my word for it, I've evidence for a conviction. This
an has never been to Lost Village. He didn't get his gold
ere. And there's no gold there, anyway, but a little
lacer stuff."

Whether they heard me or not, I don't know. They
ere all around me, yelling at me, shaking their fingers in

my face. And they were all mad. Neil was probably th
maddest of all. Marla, when I looked at her, just turne
her head away.

Feist got up when I told him to, and walked out ahea
of me. "I might have expected this," he said. "But yo
won't get away with it."

"Yes, I will. And when they discover what you tried t
put over, I'll have trouble keeping you from gettin
lynched."

When he was locked in a cell, I walked back to m
desk and sat down.

Ever feel like the whole world was against you? Wel
that's the way I felt then. My girl had turned her back o
me. The town's leading citizens—the men I'd worked fo
been friends with and protected—they all hated me. An
they could throw me out of office, that was true. All the
needed was to get the council together.

It was ten miles to the nearest telegraph, but when th
stage went out that night, I had a letter on it.

Up and down the street men were gathered in knot:
and when they looked at me they glared and muttered. S
I walked back to my office and sat down. Feist was stretche
on his cot, and he never moved.

Every night now, for months, Marla Neil had brough
me a pot of coffee at eight o'clock. When eight drew nea
I began to feel both hungry and miserable. There'd be n
Marla tonight, that was something I could bet. And ther
there she was, a little cool, but with her coffeepot.

"Marla!" I sat up straight. "Then you—?" I got t
my feet. "You're not mad at me? Believe me, Marl:
when you all know the truth, you won't be. Listen,
can ex—"

She drew back. "Drink your coffee," she said, "or
will get cold. I'll talk to you tomorrow." She turned an
hurried away.

So I sat down, ate a cookie, and then poured out th
coffee. It was black and strong, the way I like it . . . ver
black, and very strong. . . .

．　．　．

My mouth tasted funny, when I awoke, and I had trouble getting my eyes open. When I got them open I rolled and caught myself just in time. It wasn't my bed I was in. I was on a jail cot.

My head felt like it weighed a ton, but I lifted it and looked around. I was in a cell. Larik Feist's cell.

That brought me to my feet with a lurch. I charged the door.

Locked.

Taking that door in my two hands I shook it until the whole door rattled and banged. I shouted, but there was no sound from outside. I swore. Then I looked around. There was a note on the floor.

I picked it up and read:

> You wouldn't listen to us. I hated to do this, but you'd no right to keep the whole town from getting rich just because of your pigheaded jealousy.

It didn't need any signature, for by that time I was remembering that the last thing I had done was drink some coffee Marla had brought me.

The door rattled and I yelled, but nobody answered. I went to the window and looked out. Nobody was stirring, but I knew all those who lived in town weren't gone. They probably had orders to ignore me.

Then I remembered something else. This jail was old and of adobe. I'd been trying for months to get the council to vote the money to make repairs. These bars— As I've said, I weigh two hundred and thirty pounds and none of it anything but bone and muscle. I grabbed those bars and bowed my back, but they wouldn't stir. Yet I knew they weren't well seated. Then I picked up the cot and smashed it, and taking one of the short iron pieces, I used it as a lever between the bars. That did the trick.

In five minutes I was on the street, then back inside

after my guns. This time I belted on two of them, grabbe
my Winchester, and ran for the livery stable.

Abel was there, but no Wright. I grabbed Abel. "Whic
way did they go?" I yelled at him.

"Lou!" he protested, pulling back. "You let go of me.
ain't done nothing! And you leave those folks alone. We a
going to be rich."

I dropped him, because I remembered something ver
suddenly. Larik Feist had changed his clothes after h
came to town. Had he taken the old ones with him afte
he got a complete outfit? I made a run for Powers' store
but it was closed. I put one foot against the door jamb an
took the knob in my hands— It came loose, splinterin
the jamb.

The clothes were there. A worn, dirty shirt, jean:
boots, and a coat. Right there I sat down and looked the
over.

Not that I didn't know where they were going now
The Sierra Madres were far south of the border, an
nobody except a few Indians and Mexicans who live ther
knew them better than I. What I wanted to know wa
where Feist had come from, because one thing I knew
He had not come up from Mexico.

From our town the country slopes gradually away t
the Border. It's a long valley running deep into Mexico
and from my usual seat at the jail door I could look dow
that valley. Yesterday, before Feist appeared, I had bee
sitting there, and Larik Feist had not come up that valley
Nothing bigger than a mouse or rattlesnake had bee
moving out there.

Now, just before noon, Luke Fair drove his buckboar
in from Tombstone, and he had seen nobody for fift
miles, he said. The fact remained, all things considered
the only way Feist could have come was by train. Th
railroad was just ten miles away. And I'd spotted soot o
his ears, which he'd not washed off.

The dust on his clothes was not desert dust—no mor
than he could have picked up coming from the railroad

ıd there were some cinders in the cuffs of his jeans. All
s clothes were old except for the coat. It had a label from
El Paso store.

Tracking that party into Mexico offered no problem,
ıt I had another idea. Feist, if I was right, and I was
:tting my shirt on it, would get his hands on the money
at had been put up. Then he would light out and leave
em stranded. And I had just a hunch where he would
).

Luke Fair was in front of his shack when I walked up.
ou played hob," he said.

I spoke fast: "Luke, get a horse and a couple of pack
ıles. Take grub and plenty of water. Then light out after
at bunch. By the time you get to them, they'll be
ighty glad to see you."

Luke looked at me. The fact that he was here and not
ıth them showed he had brains. "What do you mean?"

"I mean," I said, "that about fifty miles south of the
ırder you'll find that bunch. They'll probably be out of
ıter and afoot."

He took his pipe out of his mouth. "I don't get you."

"That Feist," I said, "was a swindler. He never saw the
erra Madres. I'd bet a coon he never. He rigged that
ıry, and that gold never came from Lost Village because
ere's no gold there, and never was."

"How do you know that?"

"Luke, what was my ma's name?"

"Why"—he looked sort of odd—"it was Ibañez."

"Sure, and Luke, do you know what the name of that
ficer was who went with the Franciscan friars?"

"No."

"It was Ibañez. Luke, I've had a map to Lost Village
·er since I was six. My father went there when he was a
·y. I went there, too. There was a village, but folks left it
ıen the springs went dry. There never was any mining
ıse by. The mine they took the gold from was ten miles
ım the village itself, and it's being worked right now by
e Sonora Mining Company."

"Well, I'll be blasted!" Luke just sat there looking me. "Why didn't you tell them?"

"I started to, but they wouldn't listen. Most of it didn't want to tell until the trial. I didn't want this gent know what he was facing. I had no idea they'd go off th way they did."

"If I was you," he said, "I'd let 'em get back the be they can."

"They might not get back," I told him, but he kne that as well as I did. He got up and began gathering h duffel.

"What about you?" he asked.

That made me grin. "Luke, that gent will head for Paso unless I'm clean off my rocker. He'll ditch the about the second day out and he'll head through the hi toward El Paso. He'll take a straight route, and abo noon of the second day after he leaves them, he'll stop f water at a little *pozo*, a place called Coyote Spring. An Luke, when he gets there, I'll be sitting close by."

If you look on a good big map, and if you pick a pla about midway between the Animas and the Alamo Hua Mountains, and then measure off about twenty-eight mil or so south of the border, you'll find Pozo de Coyote.

The spring is in a plain, but the country is roug and broken, and the ground slopes off a little into sort of hollow. The *pozo* is in the bottom. At noo on the second day after I figured Larik Feist would hav left them, I was sitting back in the brush with my fie glasses and a rifle.

He was more than an hour late getting to the *pozo*, b I was taking it easy back in a tall clump of cholla an mesquite when I heard his horse. It was hot—a sti blazing noon in the desert when he drew up at the wat hole. Lifting my Winchester, I put a bullet into the san at his feet. He jerked around and jumped for his rifle, b as he lifted it, I smashed two shots at the stock and l dropped it as if it was hot. The stock was splintered. He stood stock-still, his hands lifted.

Getting to my feet, I walked down the hill. Once he made a motion as if to go for his gun, but I fired the rifle from the hip and grooved the leather of his holster. When I stepped into the open we were thirty yards apart.

His face was flushed with heat and fury, and he glared at me, the hatred a living thing in his eyes. "You, is it? I might have guessed."

"What kept you so long, Feist?" I said. "I've been waiting for you."

"How'd you get here? How'd you know I'd be coming this way?"

"Simple." I smiled at him, taking my time. Then I let him have it, about the map I had, how the Lost Village was not lost, and how there was no mine at all there, and no gold, and never had been.

"So you knew all the time?" It made him furious to think that. "Now what are you going to do?"

"Take you in. I wired Tucson about you. They are checking with other places. You'll be wanted some place." My rifle tilted a little. "Drop your gun belts," I told him. "Or, if you feel lucky, try to draw."

Gingerly, he moved his hands to his belt buckle, and unfastening it, he let the belt drop. Then, stepping carefully, he moved away. I closed in and picked up the belt, then shucked shells from the gun, and stuck the belt and gun in my saddlebag. Then I spoke again to Larik Feist: "Now get ready to travel, fellow."

Three days later I rode into town with Larik Feist tied to his saddle. He had made one break to escape, and had taken a bad beating. His eyes were swollen shut and his beard matted with blood and sand. He looked like he had been dragged through a lava bed on his face.

There was nobody in sight. Soon a few people, mostly women, came to the doors to watch.

Luke Fair strolled out finally. I handed him the pouch containing the money I'd recovered.

"Where's everybody? Did you find 'em?"

Fair grinned at me. "Found 'em just like you said, afoot and out of water. He'd stolen their horses and canteens, but I rounded up the horses that he'd turned loose and we started back."

"But where are they?"

He chuckled. "Mining," he said. "Working one of the richest ledges I ever saw. We started back, but about ten miles below the border, Powers sits down for a rest and crumbles a piece of rotten quartz, and it was fairly alive with gold. So they all staked claims an' they all figure that they're going to get rich."

He started to walk toward the bank, then stopped. "Marla's in town," he said.

When I'd jailed Feist, I thought about it. Suddenly, I knew what I was doing. The law could have Feist and they could have their marshal's job.

Marla opened the door for me, and she'd never looked prettier. Some of it was last-minute fixin'—I could easily see that.

My badge was in my hand. "Give that to your dad," I said. "He and Powers wanted a new marshal—now they can get him."

"But they were angry, Lou!" she protested. "They weren't thinking!"

"Be the same way next time. Feist is in jail. You can turn him over to the law, or hang him, or let him rot there, or turn him loose, for all of me."

Marla looked at me. She didn't know what to say. She was pretty and she knew it, but suddenly that meant nothing at all to me and she saw it. And believe me, it was the only thing she had, the only weapon and the only asset. I could see that then, which I couldn't see before.

"Where are you going?" she asked, hesitantly.

My horse was standing there and I stepped into the
saddle. "Why," I said, "I've been setting here since I was
a kid talking to folks who'd been places. Once I made a
trip to Tombstone, but this time, I'm really traveling. I'm
going clear to Tucson!"

So I rode out of town, and I never looked back.
Not once.

That
Packsaddle Affair

■————————■————————■

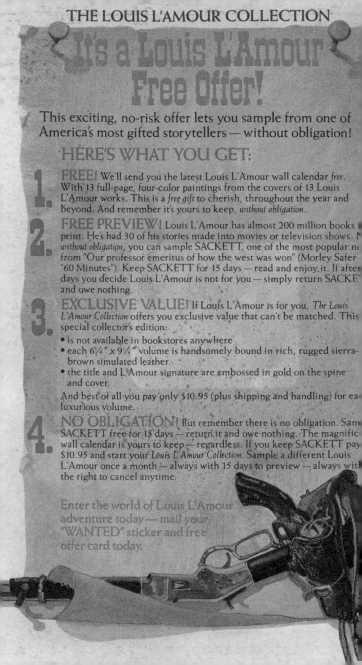

THE LOUIS L'AMOUR COLLECTION

It's a Louis L'Amour Free Offer!

This exciting, no-risk offer lets you sample from one of America's most gifted storytellers — without obligation!

HERE'S WHAT YOU GET:

1. FREE! We'll send you the latest Louis L'Amour wall calendar *free*. With 13 full-page, four-color paintings from the covers of 13 Louis L'Amour works. This is a *free gift* to cherish, throughout the year and beyond. And remember it's yours to keep, *without obligation*.

2. FREE PREVIEW! Louis L'Amour has almost 200 million books in print. He's had 30 of his stories made into movies or television shows. Now *without obligation*, you can sample SACKETT, one of the most popular no[ ] from "Our professor emeritus of how the west was won" (Morley Safer "60 Minutes"). Keep SACKETT for 15 days — read and enjoy it. If after [ ] days you decide Louis L'Amour is not for you — simply return SACKE[ ] and owe nothing.

3. EXCLUSIVE VALUE! If Louis L'Amour is for you, *The Louis L'Amour Collection* offers you exclusive value that can't be matched. This special collector's edition:

• is not available in bookstores anywhere
• each 6⅛" x 9¼" volume is handsomely bound in rich, rugged sierra-brown simulated leather.
• the title and L'Amour signature are embossed in gold on the spine and cover.

And best of all you pay only $10.95 (plus shipping and handling) for ea[ ] luxurious volume.

4. NO OBLIGATION! But remember there is no obligation. Sam[ ] SACKETT free for 15 days — return it and owe nothing. The magnific[ ] wall calendar is yours to keep — regardless. If you keep SACKETT pay[ ] $10.95 and start your *Louis L'Amour Collection*. Sample a different Louis L'Amour once a month — always with 15 days to preview — always wit[ ] the right to cancel anytime.

Enter the world of Louis L'Amour adventure today — mail your "WANTED" sticker and free offer card today.

FREE — MAGNIFICENT WALL CALENDAR!
FREE — PREVIEW OF SACKETT
- No Obligation!   - No Purchase Necessary!

Yes! I'm claiming my reward!

Send SACKETT for 15 days free! If I keep this volume, I will pay just $10.95 plus shipping and handling. Future Louis L'Amour Westerns will be sent to me about once a month, on a 15-day, Free-Examination basis. I understand that there is no minimum number of books to buy, and I may cancel my subscription at any time. The Free Louis L'Amour wall calendar is mine to keep even if I decide to return SACKETT.

NAME _____

ADDRESS _____

CITY _____

STATE _____ ZIP _____

MY NO RISK GUARANTEE:

There's no obligation to buy. The free calendar is mine to keep. I may preview SACKETT and any other Louis L'Amour book for 15 days. If I don't want it, I simply return the book and owe nothing. If I keep it, I pay only $10.95 (plus postage and handling).

70136   IL 123

"WANTED!" STICKER GOES HERE

Track down and capture exciting western adventure from one of America's foremost novelists!

• It's free! • No obligation! • Exclusive value

Author's Note

One of the things you didn't do in the West was bother a woman. It rarely happened.

Women were scarce and valued accordingly. A lot of men grew up reading the novels of Sir Walter Scott and they adopted the author's notions of chivalry. There are many, many accounts in diaries and elsewhere of women traveling back and forth across the West alone and never being disturbed in the least.

If a woman got off a stage at a stage-stop to get something to eat, and a man didn't get up to give her a place at the table, somebody else knocked him off the seat so she could be seated. You couldn't even bump into a woman walking in the street without somebody knocking you into the ground for it.

Women were treated with great respect and this was universal all over the frontier. It was one thing you didn't transgress.

Red Clanahan, a massive man
with huge shoulders and a wide-jawed face, was no longer
in a hurry. The energetic posse which had clung so persis-
ntly to his trail had been left behind on the Pecos. Their
orses had played out and two of them were carrying
ouble.

Red had pushed on to Lincoln, where he'd swapped
his sorrel for a long-legged, deep-chested black with three
white stockings. Then with only time out for a quick meal
and a changing of saddles, he'd headed west for the Rio
rande and beyond it, the forks of the Gila.

Packsaddle Stage Station was a long, low building of
dobe, an equally long, low stable, and two pole corrals.
here was a stack of last year's hay and a fenced-in pasture
where several stage horses grazed, placid in the warm
orning sun. Three saddled horses stood three-legged at
he hitch-rail, and a drowsy Mexican, already warming up
r his siesta, sat in the shade alongside the building.

Slipping the thongs from his pistol butt, Clanahan rode
own the last hundred yards to the station and dismounted
the trough. Keeping his horse between himself and the
ation, he loosened the cinch a little and then led the
orse to a patch of grass in the shade alongside the trail.
nly then did he start for the station.

A narrow-shouldered man with a thin wolf's face had
me from the stage station and was watching him. He
ore a gun butt forward in a right-side holster, which
ight be used for either the left or right hand.

"Come down the trail?" he asked, his narrow eye taking in Clanahan with cool attention.

"Part way. Came down from the Forks and across th Flat."

"Stage is late." The tall man still watched him. "Wo dered if you'd seen it?"

"No." Clanahan walked on by and opened the static door. It was cool and shadowed inside. There were sever tables, chairs, and a twenty-foot bar at which two me lounged, talking to the barkeep. Another man sat at table in the farthest corner. Both the men at the b looked rough and trail-wise.

Red Clanahan moved to the end of the bar and stoppe there where he could watch all the men and the door well. "Rye," he said, when the bartender glanced his wa

As he waited, he rested his big hands on the bar ar managed a glance toward the silent man in the corne The man just sat there with his hands clasped loosely the table, unmoving. He wore a hat that left only h mouth and chin visible at this distance and in this ligh He wore a string tie and a frock coat.

There was a situation here that Red could not fathor but he realized he had walked into something happeni or about to happen—probably connected with the arriv of the stage.

The man from outside came back in. His hips we wider than his shoulders and the holster gave him a pec liarly lopsided appearance.

Red Clanahan had a shock of red hair and a red-brow face with cold green eyes above high, flat cheekbone Once seen, he was not easily forgotten, for he was six fe three and weighed an easy two hundred and thirty pound And there were places where he was not only known, b wanted.

There was a matter of some cattle over in Texas. Red father had died while he was away, and when he returne he found that the three thousand head his father ha tallied, shortly before his death, had mysteriously bee absorbed by two larger herds. With no legal channels of recovery open to him, Red had chosen illegal methods, and one thing had led to another. Red Clanahan was high on the list of men wanted in Texas.

He finished his drink and had another. Then he looked over at the bartender. "How about some grub?"

The bartender was a big man, too, with a round face and two chins but small, twinkling eyes and a bald head. He removed his cigar and nodded. "When the stage comes in—'most any time."

The two men turned to look at him. Then the tall man looked around at the bartender. "Feed him now, Tom. Maybe he wants to ride on."

Red glanced up, his cold green eyes on the speaker. "I can wait," he said coolly.

One of the other men turned. He was short and thick-set, with a scar on his jaw. "Maybe we don't want you to wait," he said.

Red Clanahan looked into the smaller man's eyes for a long, slow minute. "I don't give a royal damn what you want," he said quietly. "Whatever you boys are cookin', don't get it in my way or I'll bust up your playhouse."

He reached for the bottle and drew it nearer as the short man started toward him. "Listen, you—"

He came one step too close and Red Clanahan hit him across the mouth with the back of his big hand. The blow seemed no more than a gesture but it knocked the shorter man sprawling across the room, his lips a bloody pulp.

Red met the gaze of the other men without moving or turning a hair. "Want in?" he said. "I'm not huntin' trouble but maybe you're askin' for it."

The tall man with the narrow shoulders looked ugly. "You swing a wide loop, stranger. Perhaps you're cuttin' into something too big for you."

"I doubt it."

His cool assurance worried Ebb Fallon. They had a job to do, and starting a fight with this stranger was no way to do it. Who was the man? Fallon stared at him, trying to remember. He was somebody, no doubt about that.

Shorty Taber got up slowly from the floor. Still dazed he touched his fingers to his crushed lips and stared at the blood. Pure hatred was in his eyes as he looked up at Clanahan.

"I'll kill you for that," Taber said.

Red Clanahan reached for the bottle and filled his glass. "Better stick to punchin' cows," he said. "Quit goin' around pickin' fights with strangers. You'll live longer."

Taber glared at him and his right hand dropped a fraction. Red was looking at him, still holding the bottle. "Don't try it," he warned. "I could take a drink and shoot both your ears off before you cleared leather."

Taber hesitated, then turned and walked to his friends. They whispered among themselves for a few minutes while the bartender polished a glass. Through it all the man at the table had not moved. In the brief silence there was a distant pounding of hoofs and a rattle of wheels.

Instantly, two of the three turned to the door. The third stepped back and dropped into a chair near the wall but facing the door. The bartender looked nervously at Red Clanahan. "We'll serve grub when the passengers arrive," he said. "They change teams here."

The stage drew up out front and then the door opened. Two men and a woman came in, and then a girl. She was slender and tall, with large violet eyes. She looked quickly toward the bar. Then her eyes touched fleetingly on Red's face, and she went on to the table and seated herself there. Obviously, she was disturbed.

Red Clanahan saw her eyes go to the third of the three riders, the fattish man who had remained indoors. Red happened to turn his head slightly and was shocked by the expression on the bartender's face. He was dead-white and his brow was beaded with sweat.

The passengers ate quietly. Finally the driver came in, had a drink, and turned. "Rolling!" he called. "Let's go!"

All got to their feet, and as they did, Ebb Fallon

walked to the door, standing where the passengers had to brush him to get by. The girl was last to leave. As she turned to the door, the man at the nearby table got up.

"All right, Ebb," he said, "tell 'em to roll it."

He moved toward the girl. "My name's Porter, ma'am. You'd best sit down."

"But I've got to get on, the stage!" she protested indignantly. "I can't stay."

She started past him and Porter caught her wrist. "Came to see your father, didn't you?" the man said. "Well, he's here."

That stopped her. Outside, the stage was in motion; then they heard it go down the trail. When the rumble of wheels had died away, the door of the station opened, and Taber stepped in. He looked at the bartender, then at Red. His eyes shifted on to the girl.

"Well, where is he?" she demanded.

Ebb Fallon lifted his hand and pointed to the man seated at the table in the corner. But before the girl could move, the bartender put one hand on the bar. "Ma'am," he said, his voice strangely gentle, "don't go to that man. They are tryin' to trick you. They want the claim."

"But, I—" She looked from one to the other. "I don't understand."

Fallon had turned on the bartender, and as he looked across the hardwood at him, his eyes were devilish. "I'll kill you for that, Sam."

"Not while I'm here," Red Clanahan said.

Fallon's face turned dark. "You keep out of this!" he lared. "Be glad you got off so easy before!"

Red continued to lean on the bar. "Ma'am," he said, "I've no idea what this is all about, but I'm your friend."

The girl turned sharply and went to the man in the corner. Yet as her hand touched him, he fell slowly forward, his hat rolling to the floor. He slumped on the table, his cheek against the table top. His eyes were wide and staring. Over one eye was a blue hole.

She stared back in horror. "Dan! That's Dan Moore, Daddy's friend!"

"That *was* Dan Moore," Fallon replied. "You come with us, ma'am."

Fallon started toward her and she shrank back. Shorty Taber and Porter turned suddenly on the bartender and Red. "Just stay where you are, you two. This girl goes with us. She'll be all right," he added. "We just want some information and then she can go on her way."

Red Clanahan straightened at the bar and reached for the bottle. Coolly, he poured a drink. "You're wastin' your time," he said patiently. "She doesn't know anything about it and never did."

Ebb Fallon turned sharply. "What's that? What did you say?"

"You heard me right. She knows nothing about the claim. Whoever hired you sure picked the dumbest help he could find. First you kill the one man who could help you; then you risk hell by kidnapin' this girl off that stage. And she not knowin' a thing!"

He looked from Fallon to Porter, his eyes cold with contempt. "Ever stop to think what'll happen when that stage reaches the end of the line and that driver finds she was taken off here? If you recall, western folks don't take to men troublin' women." He filled his glass. "I look to see you hang."

"Who are you?" Fallon persisted. "What do you know about this?"

"Who I am doesn't matter," Red replied, "except that I'm tougher than the three of you and would admire to prove it. But I'll tell you this: you did a blundering job of killing this girl's father. He wasn't dead when you left him."

"*What?*" Fallon's face was livid. "What's that?"

"I said he wasn't dead. He got into a saddle and rode all of ten miles before he passed out. He was a game man. I found him on the trail, cared for him—sat with him until he died. That was about daybreak this mornin'."

"I don't believe it!" Taber burst out. "You're lyin'!"

Clanahan glanced at Taber. "Do you want to get slapped 'ound some more? I'd enjoy doin' it."

Taber stepped back, his gun barrel lifting. "You try it!" e snarled. "I'll kill you!"

Red ignored him. "Her pa told me about the claim. old me where it was, all about it." He smiled. "Fact is, I as there this mornin', and if you want to talk business, et your boss down here with some cash."

"Cash?"

"I'm sellin' my information," Red replied, "for fifteen ousand dollars."

"But that claim belongs to the girl!" the bartender 'otested.

"Not if they get down there first and change the stakes d filin' notice." Red Clanahan shrugged, and gave Sam a lf smile. "You get your boss down here with some oney."

They hesitated, not liking it. Yet Red could see that ey were worried. The blunders they had made were w obvious to them, and there was a good chance the girl d not know where the claim was. "Don't trust him," ber said. "There's something fishy about this."

Clanahan chuckled. "You boys figure it out, but be st. I don't have much time. If it wasn't for that, I'd stay d work the claim for a while, myself. As it is, I can't stay at long."

Fallon turned on him, suddenly aware. "You're on the dge!"

"Maybe."

Through it all, the girl sat quiet, numbed by the shock her father's death and only vaguely aware these men ere bartering her future. Sam looked trapped. He was lishing the same glass for the third time, his face pale d perspiring. But what could he do? What could any e man do? His one possible ally had failed him.

"You hurry," Red told them. "My information is for le."

At that the girl looked up. "And you said you were n
friend!" she said bitterly. "You're as bad as they are!"

Red shrugged. "Worse, in some ways. Sure, I'm yo
friend. I won't see you hurt or abused, but, lady, fiftee
thousand is a lot of money! Your father refused a milli
for that claim."

"Stay here," Fallon said suddenly. "I'll go."

"No, you stay here," Porter interrupted. "I'll talk
him." He turned and went out of the door.

Clanahan glanced at the bartender. "Have the co
pack me some grub." He tossed a couple of silver dolla
on the bar, and as the bartender reached for them, R
spread out two of his fingers, indicating two lunches. On
Sam could see the signal. He picked up the money a
went back to the kitchen.

Shorty Taber crossed to the bar. His lips were swolle
Although the bleeding had stopped, his shirt was spotte
with blood and his mouth split and bruised. He took
drink and then swore as the liquor bit sharply at the ra
cuts. He glared viciously at Clanahan, who studious
ignored him.

Red picked up his glass and walked to the girl's tabl
never turning his back to the room. He sat down abrupt
and said under cover of the movement: "Everything's
right. Main thing is to get you out of here."

Her eyes were cold. "After you've all robbed me? A
murdered my father?" Her lips trembled.

Hastily, he said, "He was all right at the end, ma'ar
He really was. Passed away, calm and serene."

Silence hung in the room and Red felt his own wea
ness creeping up on him. It seemed a long time since l
had slept. The chase had been long and he had spe
endless hours in the saddle. His head nodded, then jerke
and his eyes were open. Shorty Taber was staring at hir
his eyes gleaming with malice.

Red Clanahan turned to the girl. "I'm dead from slee
When you hear a horse, wake me. Don't let them con
near me. If they start to edge nearer, push me."

Almost at once, his head was over on the table on his
~ms. Elaine McClary sat very still, her hands on the table
·fore her. Carefully, she kept her mind from any thought
‘ her father. She dared not give way to grief. For the first
ne she began to be aware of her situation.

She had used almost her last money to get here to
·eet her father after his letter about the rich strike. She
.d not worried, because he had told her he had become a
ch man. There was no one to whom she could now turn.
~e was alone. She was stranded. The one thing of value
·r father had managed to acquire was the claim and she
.d no idea where it was. Apparently nobody knew but
.e big red-headed man beside her.

She glared at him, seeing the rusty red curls around
~s ears, the great leonine head, the massive shoulders.
~e had never seen any man with so much sheer physical
·wer and strength. The size of his biceps was enormous
· her eyes, and she remembered, with a queer little
.art, those cold green-gray eyes. Yet, had they been so
·ld?

A board creaked and her head turned swiftly. Taber
·as moving toward them. "Stay back," she said, "or I'll
·ake him."

Ebb Fallon looked up. "Shorty!" he snapped angrily.
·tay away from there! If anything happens to him, where
· we stand?"

Taber turned with angry impatience and went back to
·e bar. "You weren't the one he hit," he said sullenly.

"Take your time," Fallon said. "This show ain't over
·t."

Minutes went slowly by, and the big man beside her
·pt heavily. Several times he sighed and muttered in his
·ep, and what she could see of his face was curiously
·laxed and peaceful. His sun-faded shirt smelled of old
·eat and dust, and now that she was closer to him, she
·uld sense the utter and appalling weariness of the man.
·e dust of travel was on him, and he must have come far.

"Look, ma'am." Fallon seated himself at a nearby table

and spoke softly, reasonably. "Maybe we've gone at th all wrong. I admit we want that claim, but maybe we ca make a dicker, you and us. Maybe we can do busines Now the way things shape up, you'll get nothin' for th claim. You could use money, I bet. You make a deal wi us, and you won't lose it. You sell us your interest ar we'll give you five hundred dollars."

"That claim is worth a million or more," she answere "Father refused that for it, he said."

"But you don't know where it is. Think of that. Accor ing to law, you have to do assessment work on a claim; much every year to hold it. Well, if you don't do yo work, the claim is lost anyway. How can you do it if y don't know where it is?"

Elaine shifted a little in her chair. All this was tru and it had already fled through her mind. She was helpless. If there were only— If she could talk to Sam!

"I'll have to think about it," she said. "But what can do?"

"Sign a bill of sale on that claim, and get the b hombre's gun. You're right beside it. All you have to do take it. That hombre's an outlaw anyway, ma'am. He sell you out."

But they had murdered her father! She couldn't forg that. They had not even troubled to deny it.

Her eyes lifted and she saw Sam give her a fai negative shake of the head. "I'll think about it," she stalle

If she took his gun, what then? They would kill th man as they had her father. Did that matter to he Suddenly, she remembered! This big, lonely man besi her, this very tired big man, he had trusted her. He ha asked her to help. Then, like a tired boy he had put dow his head and slept among a bunch of murderers, trusti to her to warn him.

How soon would the mysterious boss be back? How f. had Porter to go? How much time did she have?

Suppose *she* had the gun? Then she would be in bargaining position herself! They would have to listen

·r. But could she force the big man to talk? She knew
at would be impossible for her. But not, she thought
en, impossible for these other men. She read correctly
e bitter hatred in Taber's eyes.

Frightened and alone, she sat in the lonely stage sta-
·n and watched the hard, strange faces of these men she
d never seen until scarcely an hour before. Now these
·angers suddenly meant life and death to her.

She looked down at her hands, listening to the bar-
nder put down a glass on the back bar and take up
other. Then she heard a faint drumming of horses' hoofs,
d suddenly—why she would never know—she sprang
her feet, drawing the big red-headed man's gun as she
·d so and stepping back quickly.

Almost as suddenly, and catlike, wide-awake where a
cond before he had been sleeping, the big man was back
ainst the wall. He stared at her, then around the room.
·ive me that gun!" he said hoarsely.

"No."

Shorty Taber laughed suddenly, triumphantly. "How
you like it this way, Big Boy? Now look who's in the
ddle!"

"Let me have the gun, ma'am," Fallon said reasonably.
ll take it now."

She stepped back again. "No. Don't any of you come
ar me."

Her eyes caught the shocked horror in the bartender's
·es and doubt came to her. Had she done wrong? Should
e have awakened the big man? She heard the horses
aw up, heard two men dismount.

Porter entered, then another man—a big, wide-faced
an with a tawny, drooping mustache and small, cunning
·ue eyes. He took in the tableau with a quick glance,
·en smiled.

His eyes went slowly to Clanahan. "Well, friend, looks
·e you weren't in such a good spot to bargain. Do you
·ow where that claim is?"

"I sure do," Red snapped. Out of the corner of his

mouth, he said to the girl: "Give me that gun, you litt
fool!"

"If she does, I'll shoot her," Taber said. "I never shot
woman yet, but so help me, I will. I'll shoot her, and the
you."

"Shootin' a woman would be about your speed, Shorty
Red's tone was contemptuous. "Ever tackle a full-grow
man?"

Shorty's nostrils flared and he swung his gun. "
the—"

"*Taber!*" The big man with the tawny mustache took
step forward. "You shoot and I'll kill you myself! Don't
a fool!"

There was a short, taut silence. "Now, Red," the b
man said quietly, "we can do business. Looks to me li
you're on the dodge. I saw your horse out there. A migh
fast horse, and it's come far and hard. I know that hors
It's from the Ruidoso, over in Lincoln County. Unless y
knew that outfit well, you'd never have it. And if they
you have it, you're an outlaw."

"So?"

Red Clanahan stood very still, his big feet apart,
eyes wary and alert. Like a photograph, that room wi
every chair, table, and man was in his mind.

"So we can do business," the tawny-mustached m
said. "Tell me where that claim is and I'll give you
thousand dollars."

Red chuckled. "You foolin'?"

"You better." The newcomer was casual. "If you don
you'll never get out of here alive. Nor will the girl."

They faced Red and the girl, who were seven or eig
feet apart. Fallon was closest to her. Porter and the bo
were nearest to Red.

"And you'd lose a million dollars." Red grinned tightl
"You make me smile. How many men are crawlin' ov
these hills now, lookin' for lost mines? How many w
always be doin' it? Mister, you know and I know there
nothin' so lost as a lost mine. Gold once found is migh

y about bein' found again. If you kill me, you haven't
e chance in a million of findin' that gold."

"We could make him talk," Shorty suggested.

Red Clanahan laughed. "You think so? You little coy-
e, you couldn't make a ten-year-old kid talk. The Apaches
orked on me for two days once, and I'm still here."

The boss eyed him. "Who are you, Red? Seems I
ight to know you."

"You wouldn't, only by hearsay. I run with the lobos,
ot with coyotes."

The boss seemed to tighten and his eyes thinned down.
ou use that word mighty free. Suppose we work on the
rl? I wonder how fast you'd talk then?"

Red Clanahan shrugged. "How would that hurt me?
he's a pretty kid, but I never saw her before she walked
here. She's nothing in my life. You torture her and all
ou'd get would be the trouble of it. You'd be surprised
ow I could bear up under other people's trouble."

"He ain't as tough as he looks," Taber said. "Let's work
the girl."

"No," the boss said, "I don't—" His voice broke off.
ome of Red's relief must have shown in his eyes, for the
oss suddenly changed his mind. "Why, yes, Shorty, I
ink we will. You take—"

The girl's gun seemed to waver, and Fallon grabbed
r it. Instantly, the girl fired and Red Clanahan lunged.

He was cat-quick. With a bound he was half across the
om. His shoulder struck Porter and knocked him ca-
ening into the boss, and both fell against the bar. Red's
ove had the immediate effect of turning all the fire away
om the girl, shifting the center of battle. But his lunge
rried him into a table and he fell over a chair. Yet as he
t the chair his big hand emerged from under his shirt
ith a second gun.

Fallon was struggling with the girl, and Red's first
llet caught Shorty in the midriff. Shorty took a step
ck, his eyes glazing. Guns exploded and flame stabbed.
ed lunged to his feet, moving forward, swaying slightly,

spotting his shots carefully, the acrid smell of gunpowde in his nostrils. Then suddenly the room was still.

Only the boss was on his feet and Fallon was steppin away from the girl, his hands lifted. The boss had bloo trickling from his left shoulder. Shorty Taber was dow his eyes wide and empty.

Porter was slumped against the bar, a gun beside h hand, the front of his vest dark with blood, which w forming a pool under him.

Red moved swiftly and gathered up his second gu from where it had fallen. "Fifteen thousand, boss," he sa quietly, "and I'll tell you what I know. I'll give you th map the girl's father drew for me." Red Clanahan holstere one gun. "Act fast," he said. "I haven't much time."

Sam looked at the boss. "You want me to get it out the safe, Johnson?"

Johnson's voice was hoarse. He clutched his bloo shoulder. "Yeah." Then he begged. "Let me get my shou der fixed. I'll bleed to death."

"Afterwards." Clanahan watched Sam go to the saf "Johnson own this place, Sam?"

"Uh-huh."

"Looks like you're through here, then."

"You're tellin' me?" Sam brought two sacks to th counter. "They'd kill me after this."

"Then go saddle two horses. One for yourself and on for the lady."

"Miss," Clanahan gestured to her, "write him out a b of sale to the claim designated on that map."

"But—" Elaine started a protest, then stifled it Red's sudden impatience.

"Hurry!" he said angrily. "Do what I tell you!"

Red Clanahan saw Sam come around the building wit the saddled horses, and yelled at him: "Tie Fallon," h said. "But let Johnson alone. By the time he gets Fallo loose and that shoulder fixed, we'll be too far off. And if h follows, we'll kill him."

Johnson took the map and the bill of sale, smilin

ddenly. "Maybe it was worth a bullet-shot shoulder," he
id. "That's a rich claim."

Sam picked up the gold and sacked it into the saddle
gs. Then he picked up the lunch he had packed earlier,
d two hastily filled canteens.

In the saddle, Red said hoarsely, "Ride fast now! Get
t of sight!"

Elaine glanced at him and was shocked by the sudden
llor of his face. "You! You're hurt!" she cried.

His wide face creased in a grin. "Sure! But I didn't
re let those hombres guess it. Keep goin' a few miles. I
n stick it."

Beside a stream they paused and bandaged his wound.
was a deep gouge in the side, from which he had bled
ely. He watched the girl work over it with quick, sure
gers.

"You'd do to take along, ma'am. You're sure handy."

"I worked for a doctor."

Back in the saddle, they switched off the trail and
aded up through the timber.

Sam rode beside them, saying nothing. His round face
s solemn.

"By the way," Red said, "I better tell you. I looked at
ur dad's claim. And he was wrong, ma'am. It wasn't
rth a million. It wasn't worth scarcely anything."

Shocked, she looked around at him. "What do you
an?"

"Your dad struck a pocket of free gold. It was richer
an all get-out, but your dad was no minin' man. There
't a thousand dollars left in that pocket."

"Then—"

"Then if you'd kept it, you'd have had nothing but
rd work and nothin' more. You got fifteen thousand."

"But I thought—"

Red chuckled. "Ma'am," he said, "I never stole from
woman. I just figured those hombres wanted that claim
bad, they should have it."

■　　■　　■

Cresting the divide, two days later, they saw the smo‚ of a far-off town. Red Clanahan drew up. "I leave y‚ here. My trail," he pointed north, "goes that way. Y‚ take her to town, will you, Sam?"

The older man nodded. "Where are you headed, Re‚ The Roost?"

Clanahan glanced at him, wry humor in his eyes.

"Yeah. You know me?"

"Sure. I seen you once before, in Tascosa."

Clanaham glanced briefly at the girl. "Take it easy wi‚ that money, ma'am." He lifted a hand. "So long."

The flanks of the horse gleamed black a time or t‚ among the trees.

Elaine stared after him, her eyes wide and tear-fille‚

"He—he is a good man, isn't he?" she said softly.

"Yeah, a real good man," Sam answered.

"What did you mean? The Roost?"

Sam rode on in silence; then he said, "Robber's Roo‚ ma'am. It's a hangout for outlaws up in the Utah cany‚ country. The way he rode will take him there."

"You knew him?"

"By sight, ma'am. His name's Red Clanahan, and th‚ say he's killed nineteen men. It's said that he is a r‚ badman."

"A good badman," she said, and looked again at whe‚ the horse had vanished in the trees. Once, far on a blu‚ misted ridge she thought she saw movement, a rid‚ outlined briefly on the horizon. And then it was gone.

She might have been mistaken.

Showdown
on the Tumbling T

Author's Note

A man who was a gunfighter was simply a man who was good with a gun. His skill was usually the result of very steady nerves, very good reactions, and good coordination. A man might have had no intention of being a gunfighter at all, but then he got into a disagreement with somebody, and because of his ability, he was faster with a gun and he won. After he won two or three times he had a reputation as a gunfighter, whether he wanted it or not.

Very few gunfighters wanted to be known as such. The notion that a man went around trying to outdraw other people in order to build a big reputation seldom ever happened, unless they were either very young boys or somebody who was a psychopathic case.

Guns were dangerous and these men knew it. They carried guns because they were a tool of their living. You had to have them for many reasons aside from just wanting to shoot somebody else.

Chapter I
Death Trap

Under the slate-gray sky the distant mountains were like a heap of rusty scrap iron thrown helter-skelter along the far horizon. Nearby, the desert was the color of pink salmon and scattered with the gray of sagebrush and a few huddles of disconsolate greasewood. The only spot of green anywhere in sight was the sharp, strong green of tall pines in a notch of the rust-red mountains.

That was the place I'd come from Texas to find, the place where I was to hole up until Hugh Taylor could send word for me. It was something to have a friend like Hugh, someone to give you a hand up when the going was rough. When I had returned from Mexico to find myself a fugitive from justice, he had been the only one to offer help.

A few scattered drops of rain pounded dust from the desert. I dug into my pack for my slicker. By the time I had it on the rain was coming down in a steady downpour that looked fair to last the night through as well as the afternoon.

Rowdy, my big black, was beginning to feel the hard going of the past weeks. It was the only time I had ever seen the big horse even close to weariness, and it was no wonder. We had come out of Dimmit County, Texas, to the Apache country of central Arizona, and the trails had been rough.

The red rocks of the mountains began to take on form and line, and I could see the raw cancers of washes that ate into the face of the plain, and the deep scars of canyons. Here and there lines of gray or green climbed the creases in the rock, evidence of underlying water or frequent rains among the high peaks.

The trail curved north, skirting the mountains toward the sentinel pines. "Ride right to the Tin Cup ranch," Hugh Taylor had said, "and when you get there, ask for Bill Keys. He'll be in charge, and he'll fix you up until this blows over. I'm sure I can get you cleared in a short time."

The mountains cracked wide open on my left and the trail turned up a slope between the pines. Blue gentians carpeted both sides of the road and crept back under the trees in a solid mass of almost sky-blue. The trail was faint, and apparently used very little, but there were tracks made by two riders and I watched them curiously. The tracks were fresh and they were headed into the Tin Cup canyon.

You can bet I had my eyes open, for even so far away from anyone that knew me there might be danger, and a man on the dodge learns to be careful.

Then I heard a shot.

It rapped out sharp and clear and final, bringing my head up with a jerk and my hand down to the stock of my Winchester. My rifle rode in a scabbard that canted back so that the stock almost touched my right thigh, and I could draw that rifle almost as fast as a man could draw a six-gun.

Rowdy heard that shot, too, and Rowdy knew what shooting could mean. He skirted the rocks that partially barred the way into the Tin Cup, and I looked down into a little valley with a stone barn and stone house, two corrals, and two riderless horses.

Then I saw the men. The air was sharp and clear, and

were only a couple of hundred yards off. There were
e of them, and one was lying on the ground. The man
stood over the body looked up and yelled at the other
near the corner of the house. "No, it ain't him!" And
a they both saw me.

Panic must have hit them both, but one of them made
eak for his horse while the other swung his hand down
his gun. Honest men don't start shooting when a
nger rides up; so as his six-gun lifted, my rifle cleared
boot. He fired, but I wasn't worried. He was much too
away.

He made a dive for his horse and I held my fire. As he
ed in the saddle I squeezed off my shot. He jerked
he was hit and I saw the gun fall from his hand into
rocks, and then they were taking out of there, but fast.
y wanted no part of my shooting.

Rowdy wasn't gun-shy. With me in the saddle he had
cause to be, after all we had been through down
xico way. That was a part of my life I never talked
ut much, and even Hugh, who was my best friend,
w nothing about it. To him I was still the quiet kid he
seen grow up on our uncle's ranch, the XY.

Rowdy was in no shape for a chase, so I let the riders
and swung down beside the old man and felt of his
se. That was mostly a matter of form. No man with that
bullet hole where he had it was going to be alive. The
shot was a bit high, and I could see there had been
e interval, for the blood around the first wound was
gulated.

A horse's hoof clicked on stone and I turned with my
ds spread. You don't pull anything fancy when four
a are looking down rifles at you.

"What did you kill him for?" The speaker was a squat,
ad-chested man with a square red face and gimlet eyes.
looked tough as a winter in the mountains, and at least
of the riders with him looked fit to side with the devil
a ride through hell.

"Don't jump your fences, pardner," I told him, pretty

chilly. "I didn't shoot this gent. When I rode into the (two hombres were standing here, one right over h They took a shot at me, then lit out, ridin' up the valle I came in."

"We heard shootin'," the square-faced man repli "He's dead an' you're here."

My eyes went over them, sizing them up. Nob needed to burn any brands on this hide for me. Her was on the dodge from one killing of which I wasn't gui and now I'd run smack-dab into another. Nobody had s those other riders but me, so what happened now pended a whole lot on just who and what these men we

At first glance I could see there was only one ma the four who would give anybody a break. He was a yo fellow with brown eyes and dark hair, and a careful loo his eyes. He looked smart and he looked honest, altho a man can be fooled on both counts.

The square-built man who had done the talking seen to be the big gee. "Who are you, anyway?" he demand "What brings you here?"

Something in the way he asked that question me get downwind of an idea. I decided to tell hombre nothing, least of all that I was Wat Bell. "W they call me the Papago Kid, and I'm from down Son way.

"As for what brings me here, it was this black ho brought me, and the trail through the pines. A lot of tr have brought me a lot of places, and"—I added this w some meaning—"when I wanted to ride out, nob stopped me."

His eyes sharpened down and his lips thinned ou could see the old devil coming up in his eyes. This n was not one you could push far. He figured he was so salty, and he had no liking for being called up to the m by any casual drifter. However, there was a funny li frown came into his eyes when I mentioned my name; somehow the idea was there, full size and ready for bra ing, that he had expected another name. That feeling

strong in me that it started me thinking about a lot of
ags.

Sometimes a man rides trails and reads sign so long
t he develops an instinct for things. There was the
ng smell of trouble in my nostrils now, and for some
son I knew that I'd made a good bet when I told him I
; the Papago Kid. The funny part of it was that if he
ld find a way to check back down the Sonora trail, he'd
l out I hadn't lied. A man sometimes can have two
nes that take separate trails, and if I was young Wat
l in Dimmit County, Texas, I was also the Papago Kid
vn in Sonora.

"Lynch," the young fellow interrupted, "let's get in
of this rain, and get the body in, too. I liked old Tom
llow, and I don't like his body lying around like this."
:n he added, "We can talk just as well over some
:ee, anyway."

Lynch hesitated, still not liking me, and itching for
play. "All right," he agreed, and turning to the other
:rs, a fat-faced man and a tall, stoop-shouldered rider,
added, "you two pick Ludlow's body up and cart it out
he stable. Cover it with a blanket and then come on in.
:ter put the horses in, too." He looked at the tall man.
:n't leave anything undone, Bill," he added.

When I heard the tall man called Bill a faint suspicion
red in me, but I didn't look up. When I did, the
man answered my question for me without any
:ing from me. "You take his feet, Keys. I'll get his
·ulders."

Lynch turned abruptly toward the door of the stone
ise and I followed with the young fellow behind me.
ide, Lynch got out of his slicker and I got a shock. He
; wearing a sheriff's badge on his vest.

"The coffee was your idea, Dolliver," Lynch suggested.
'ant to start it?"

Dolliver nodded, and I knew he had seen my reaction
:hat badge and was curious about it. He turned toward
shelves and began taking things down as if he knew

the place. In the meantime I was trying to scout my t
and read the sign of this situation I'd run into.

Hugh Taylor had told me to ride to the Tin Cup
ask for Bill Keys. Yet when I arrived here, there wa
dead man on the ground who isn't Bill Keys but is app
ently the owner of the place. Meanwhile, Keys appear
be riding for the sheriff, and with what reason I had
idea.

It was a neat little house, tidy as an old maid's boud
and the smell of coffee that soon filled the room gave
cozy, homelike feel. The fireplace was big enough, and
the cooking utensils were bright and clean. A blanket o
a door curtained off an inner room.

Lynch dropped astride a chair and began to buil
smoke. He had a bullet head covered with tight ring
and a mustache that drooped in contrast. Slinging my
on a hook, I hung up my own slicker and dropped i
another chair. Lynch saw my two guns and his face chil
a little. Something about me disturbed him, and I decid
it was partly the guns—the fact that I was wearing the
not that he feared them.

"You call yourself the Papago Kid?" Lynch's quest
was sharp.

My eyes held his and I knew Sheriff Lynch and I w
not going to be friends. He was distinctly on the prod,
he was digging for something, too. I was beginning
wonder if I didn't know what it was he wanted. "I've be
called that," I said, "and I like the name. You can use i

"Did you get a good look at those two riders who
out of here? The two you said you saw?"

"I did see them. No, the look I got wasn't too go
One of them legged it for his bronc and the other grabb
iron. Naturally, with a man drawing a gun on me, ever
that distance, I wasn't wasting any time looking him ove

"How many shots did you hear?"

"One."

Dolliver turned around from the coffee. "I heard thre

"That's right," I agreed. "One shot apparently kil

old man. Then I rounded into sight and one of these
mbres took a shot at me. I shot back." I hitched my
ir back a little. "However, as you no doubt saw, the old
n was shot twice. I figure he was wounded some place
ay from the ranch, then trailed down by the killers,
o finished the job."

"What gives you that idea?" Lynch demanded.

"If you noticed, Sheriff," I said, "the rain hadn't washed
the old man's tracks. Those tracks came from toward
corrals, and even from where I stood I could see the
man had fallen down twice on that little slope, and
re were blood spots on his clothes."

It was obvious enough that the sheriff had seen noth-
of the kind, and he studied me carefully. I was doing
ne thinking on my own hook. The reason the sheriff
In't seen those tracks was because all his attention had
en centered on me.

Dolliver, whose attitude I liked, brought the coffee up
the table and filled our cups. He was a clean-cut young-
r and no fool.

The door opened then and Bill Keys came in with his
friend. They knocked the rain from their hats and shed
ir slickers, both of them looking me over while they
re doing it. Dolliver filled cups for them and they found
airs and sat down.

It struck me as faintly curious that Sheriff Lynch was
king no effort to trail the men I had mentioned, nor to
if there were tracks to back up my story. I wondered
at Dolliver thought of that, and was glad that he was
h us. This was new country for me, and I was definitely
a bad spot, and unless the breaks came my way I'd soon
re the choice of shooting my way out or I'd find myself
king into my past through the leaves of a cottonwood
h the loop end of a rope around my neck.

"You ever been in this country before?" Lynch demanded.

"Never. When I left my home in California, I crossed
zona down close to Yuma and went into Mexico."

"How'd you happen to find this place? It ain't the

easiest valley to find." He stared at me suspiciously, eyes trying to pry behind my guileless eyes. I was wear: my most innocent face, carefully saved for just su emergencies.

"Did you ever cross that desert behind here?" I ask "The only spot of green a man can see is right he Naturally, I headed for the pines. Figured there might people where there was water."

That was simple enough even for him, and he mul over it a little. "You said you came from California? Y sound like a Texan to me."

"Hell," I grinned cheerfully, "it's no wonder! On t last spread I rode for down Mexico way there were ei, Texans. My folks spoke Spanish around home," I lied, when I talked English with that Texas outfit, naturall picked up their lingo."

The story was plausible enough, but Lynch didn't I it. He didn't get a chance to ask any more questions fo minute, as I beat him to it. "What's up, Sheriff?" I ask "Is this a posse? And if it is, why pick on me?"

Lynch didn't like that, and he didn't like me. "Hunt a Texas outlaw supposed to be headed this way," he sa grudgingly, "a murderer named Wat Bell. We got w he was headed west so we're cuttin' all the trails."

"Bad weather to be riding," I sympathized, "unl you're on a red-hot trail. Is this Bell a bad hombre? Wil take four of you?"

Dolliver's eyes were shrewd and smiling. "I'm not one them," he told me. "I have a little ranch just over the mo tain from here, and joined these boys back in the pines wh they headed this way. My ranch is the Tumbling T."

Chapter II
Puzzle on the Tumbling T

Lynch ended his questions and devoted himself to coffee. From the desultory conversation that followed wh

Lynch mulled things over, I learned that the dead man, old Tom Ludlow, had owned the Tin Cup, and had no enemies that anybody knew. Win Dolliver was his nearest neighbor, and liked the old man very much, as had his sister, Maggie Dolliver.

The nearest town was Latigo, where Sheriff Ross Lynch had his office. The fat rider was Gene Bates, but nothing more was said about Wat Bell or what made the sheriff so sure he could find him that he started out on a rainy day. Knowing the uncertainties of travel in the West, and the liking of sheriffs for swivel chairs, I had a hunch that somebody had tipped the sheriff. It was less than reasonable to suppose he would start out with two men in bad weather merely on the chance that the man he sought was coming to Arizona.

Lynch looked up suddenly. "We'll be ridin' on into Latigo," he said, "and I reckon you'd better come along."

"Are you arresting me?"

His blue eyes turned mean again. He didn't like me even a little bit. "Not necessarily," he said, "but we'll be wantin' to ask you questions, an' we'll be gettin' answers."

"Look, my friend." I leaned forward just a little, and having my hands on my hips as I did, the move put my gun butts practically in my palms. "I'm not planning to get stuck for something somebody else did. You rode down here and for some reason assumed I was the guilty man. Anyway, you're all set on taking me in.

"You made no effort, and I'll leave it to Dolliver here, to check my story. You've sat here while the rain washed or partly washed those tracks away. You made no effort to get after those killers.

"You claim you're hunting some killer named Wat Bell, yet when you got here all the ambition seemed to leave you. Mr. Sheriff, I'm not your man. I didn't kill Tom Ludlow. I never saw him before. I have all the money I need, and a better horse than any of you ride. Ludlow had nothing at all that I could want. The only shot I've fired was from my rifle, and Ludlow was shot with a pistol, and that last one was fairly close up."

Lynch looked ugly. "I know what I'm doin'!" he stated flatly. "I've got my reasons!"

This looked like a good time to let them in on something. How anxious they were for gunplay, I didn't know. I did know that I stood a much better chance right here than on the trail. I'd a sudden hunch that might be hay wire as could be, but it might be correct. I'd a hunch Lynch had been told Wat Bell was coming right to the Tin Cup. I'd a further hunch that Wat Bell was not supposed to leave this ranch alive, and also that while Lynch now had doubts that I was Wat Bell, he was very apt to gun me down once I was on the road with the three of them.

"All right!" I said, "you've got your reasons! Well, I have mine for not going into Latigo with you! I don't wear two guns just for fun, and if those two shots had been fired at Ludlow by me he'd never have come back to this ranch. If you want to call my bluff and see whether I savvy guns or not, just buy chips in my game and you'll see!"

He was madder right then than a wildcat in a swarm of bees, but he wasn't very happy about the spot he was in. Ross Lynch was not yellow, not by a jugful, but I knew there were several things about this setup he didn't like. The presence of Win Dolliver, whom I now knew had joined him by accident, was one of them. Another was the fact that I said I was the Papago Kid. That name meant nothing to him. But if, as I now believed, he had been tipped off that Wat Bell was coming to this ranch, then had confused the issue enough so that he wasn't sure who I was.

Also, he was no fool. He had seen those two guns, and the guns had seen use. If we cut our dogs loose in this cabin, somebody was going to get hurt besides me. Nobody knew that better than Lynch.

Dolliver smoothed things over. He was a smart hombre, that one. "There's something to what he says, Ross. After all, why should we suspect him? It could just a

asily have been me who found Ludlow. I was headed this
ay when I met you boys.

"We should have looked for those tracks, too. I'm
onest to say that I never thought of it." He turned to me.
Did you hit the man you shot at?"

"Burned him, I think. His horse was moving. I held
y fire, but it was the best chance I had." Right then I
ecided to say nothing about the gun the rider had dropped,
ut to have a look the first chance I got. That gun might
e a clue that would help me ferret out the answer to this
eal.

Lynch was getting ready to say something, and I was
re I wouldn't like it. Dolliver interrupted. "Look, Ross,"
e said quietly, "don't blame the Kid here for being on
e prod. You can't blame him, riding into a deal like
is. He certainly could have no reason to shoot Ludlow.
et him come on over to my place with me. I can use a
nd for a few days, and when you want to see him, ride
er. That will clear this situation up, and I think Papago
ll agree to work for me. I'll pay him top hand's wages."

"That's good for me," I agreed. "I'm not hunting trou-
e. I'll do all I can to find that killer, and if you want, I'll
y to trail those men for you. I've ridden trails before," I
ded, and I pointed this one right at Lynch, "and found
t right where they ended."

Lynch didn't like it, but no more than any other man
d he have a stomach for gunplay in that close quarters.
ne presence of Win Dolliver was a big help, and allowed
m a chance to back out and save face.

The same questions kept coming into my mind. How
d they learned Wat Bell was headed this way? Why had
ugh Taylor told me to ask for Bill Keys on the Tin Cup
nen it was owned by Ludlow? Who had killed the old
an, and why?

Bill Keys was another puzzle. Taylor had said the man
uld be trusted, but he didn't size up right to me. How
od a description did he have of me? Or did he have one
all? Hugh might not have known him so well, and could

have been mistaken in trusting him. For one, I was doin
no talking until I understood the lay of the land.

Something else had come into my mind that someho
I'd never thought of before. When Hugh Taylor had m
me that night and told me of my uncle's murder, and th
I was wanted for it, I had thought of little else. True, I h
left town rather suddenly after a quarrel with old To
Bell, but that he had been murdered on the night I left f
Mexico, I'd had no idea until then. Hugh had showed n
the reward poster, but had assured me that he did
believe me guilty. He had investigators working on t
crime, and advised me to go away and stay in hiding un
he sent for me.

My mind was full of questions. Had my uncle left
will? And to whom had he left two hundred thousa
acres of his ranch? And who *had* killed him?

Bill Keys got up and turned toward the door and r
eyes dropped to his gun, absently noting that a chip h
been broken from the bone handle, and the break look
recent. Sheriff Ross Lynch and Bates followed him o
and then Dolliver and I. When he rode around the corn
of the house, Keys was saddling a horse with which
carry the body into town.

Once around the house, I slid from the saddle a
scrambled into the rocks. A hasty look showed me on
one thing. The gun was gone!

Win Dolliver looked at me curiously, but said nothi
until we were well along the trail to the Tumbling T.
was just six miles, and Dolliver talked pleasantly a
easily of the country, the cattle, and the rain. Ludlow h
been running only about six hundred head, while he h
four times that many. Keys and Bates, holding a ranch
partnership, ran a few head over west.

When we were in sight of his own ranch, Win turne
"Did you get a good look at those riders? Enough to kn
them again?"

"No," I admitted, realizing this was the first point
question he had asked, and wondering what was behind

'but one of them lost a gun back there. When I looked it was gone."

"Maybe you just didn't find it?"

"No, I saw where it had been. There was a boot track near it."

We didn't say anything more right then because the door opened and a girl stepped out on the porch and I forgot everything I had been thinking and all that had happened.

There is no description for a girl like that. It was simply that this was the girl I had been looking for all my life. It wasn't a matter of eyes nor hair, although hers were beautiful; it was simply that here she was, the girl that was meant for me. She was trimly shaped and neat, and there was quick laughter in her eyes, and there was interest and appraisal, too.

"Mag," Dolliver said, swinging down, "meet the Papago Kid. He's riding through the country and has had a little trouble with Ross Lynch."

"That's nothing against him on the T!" Maggie Dolliver replied with spirit. "You know what I think of Ross!"

Win chuckled. "Everybody should, after the way you told him off at the last Latigo dance! But what about Howie Taber?"

She flushed, and I didn't miss that. The name struck me, too. "Who did you say?" I asked.

"Taber. He is a partner of Lynch's in a ranch they have out here. At least Taber owns the ranch and Lynch runs the cows when he's not working at being sheriff. Pretty well off, Taber is. And he made quite a play for Maggie when he was out here last."

Maggie made better coffee than Win, I found, and her cookies were wonderful. I listened mostly, and answered a few random questions about Mexico. Then I started in, and asked my first question. "What about Keys? Who is he?"

"Keys?" The question puzzled Dolliver. "Frankly, I don't like the man. He ranches some with Bates, as I said, and he and Lynch are thicker than thieves. There's a story around that he ran with that horse-stealing outfit down in the Bradshaws, but I wouldn't know how true it is. He's also supposed to be something of a gun hawk. He has killed one man I know of—a drifter in Latigo."

Maggie looked at me curiously; then a thought seemed to occur to her and she turned to Win. "What I can't understand is why anyone would want to kill a nice old man like Uncle Tom Ludlow!"

"It was a mistake," I said, repeating what I had overheard when I rode up on the killers. "I think they were looking for someone else."

"But who?" Win puzzled. "And why?"

"I think," I said deliberately, "they were looking for me. I think they saw a rider at the expected place and shot him, then finished him off to prevent him talking when they found their mistake."

"But who was it they were after?" Maggie demanded.

"Me," I repeated dryly. "I think they wanted me."

Moreover, I told myself, if they had wished to kill me and had failed, they would surely try again. Had they been sure that I was Wat Bell rather than the Papago Kid, they would have insisted I go to town with them, and shot me, "trying to escape" on the way in. As it was, probably Win Dolliver's presence had saved me at first sight.

"Don't take what I said about working too seriously," Win volunteered, after a moment. "My main idea was to get you away from Lynch without a fight. He's tough, and he didn't like you. I could see that. Dangerous as he is, I think you've more to fear from Bill Keys."

Neither of them asked me any questions, nor why I believed it had been me the killers wanted. Whatever their reason for inviting me here, and I was convinced there was a reason, they asked no questions and offered no information.

Chapter III
Papago Makes a Hand

Nevertheless, I was up at daybreak with the hands, ate breakfast with them and with Win, and rode out to work with them. Later in the morning when Maggie came out to join us, I overheard him tell her, "Whatever else he may be, Mag, he's a hand. He's done more work than any two of the regular boys."

Maybe it was because these cedar brakes were a pipe after brush-popping down in the Big Bend, where I had worked two years, but I did get a lot done. And maybe because it was good to have a rope in my hands and a cow by the tail instead of only a gun. Yet all the time I worked, my mind was busy, and it didn't like what seemed to be truth.

A lot of loose ends were beginning to find their way to a common point, and I had begun to see that in skipping out of Texas I had made a big mistake. Hugh Taylor, aside from being my cousin, was also my friend, or so I had believed. From anyone but him I would never have taken the advice he had given.

Hugh Taylor had run off from the ranch where we were growing up when he was sixteen, and returned again after four years. After being around a year, he took off again, and returned some months later with money and a silver-mounted saddle. He was bigger than I, and rugged. He was also two years older. A top hand at anything he did, he stood high in my uncle's favor.

Yet I'd worked on at the ranch, never leaving, punching cows, mending fence, riding herd. I had taken two herds north over the trail, and I'd had a gunfight in Abilene, and killed my man. I wasn't proud of that, and as only a few of the trail hands returned, and they promised not to talk, nobody around the XY knew. Later, when I was down in the Big Bend with a bunch of cattle, we had trouble with Mexican bandits, and I went into their camp,

brought back some stolen horses, and did it without firin
a shot.

Finally, when I was twenty-four, Uncle Tom and I ha
a big argument, and I got mad and lit out for Mexic
Crossing the Border, I didn't want to be known as Unc
Tom Bell's nephew, so I called myself the Papago Ki
Riding through Coahuila to Durango, I had several fight
and then, moving up into Sonora, I tied up with o
Valverdes and protected his ranch against bandits. Whi
there I had two more gunfights, one with a Mexica
gunman, the other with an American.

Then, after being away two years, I had returne
across the Border and the first person I'd met was Hug
At the time it seemed a stroke of luck, and I rememb
how startled he was to see me.

"You here, Wat?" he had exclaimed. "Don't you kno
you're wanted for murder?"

That got me, and in reply to my heated questions, I
told me that the night after our quarrel Uncle Tom ha
been shot and killed, that I was sought as the killer, but
story had returned to the XY that I had been killed I
bandits in Mexico.

"Your best bet is to get out of here," he told me. "Ri
west to Arizona. I've some friends out there, and in t
meantime I'll do what I can to straighten this up."

So my uncle was dead, and they believed I had kill
him. I hadn't, but somebody else had, and who was th
somebody? Also, what kind of a deal had Hugh sent n
into at the Tin Cup? I arrive to find a man murdered, ar
the sheriff hunting a "Texas outlaw" known as Wat Bell
and knowing exactly where to find him and when.

That last didn't make sense until I began to rememb
my last stop before getting there. It had been in Lincol
New Mexico, and I had stopped there with a frie
of Hugh Taylor's. Now if that friend had wired Sher
Lynch, and Lynch had done a little figuring as to miles
day, it would not be too hard to arrive at the day of n

rival at the Tin Cup—a sufficiently secluded spot for
.urder.

Uncle Tom Bell had no relatives anyone knew of but
ugh and myself, so he would naturally leave his two
.ndred thousand acres to us, and if one of us died, then
.e other would inherit everything. I didn't like to think
.at of Hugh, but he had been a little greedy, I remem-
.red, even as a youngster.

A few discreet inquiries around proved that nobody
.d ever heard of Hugh Taylor, yet Taylor knew people
.re, and they knew him. I was still studying about that
.hen Mag loped her pony over to where I sat my horse,
.atching the herd we'd bunched.

"Win tells me you're a hand!" she said, smiling at me.
. hope you decide to stay. He likes you, and it will be
.nesome for him after I leave."

That hit me hard. I turned in my saddle. "After you
.ave? Then you're going away?"

She must have seen something in my face because hers
.ddenly changed and the smile went out of it. "I . . . I'm
.ing to be married," she said quietly.

That was all. Neither of us had another thing to say
.;ht then. For me, she had said it all. If in all the world
.ere was a girl for me, this was the one. I wanted her as I
.ver had wanted anything. But I was just the Papago
.id, and a fugitive from the law.

What she was thinking I have no idea, but she didn't
.ok happy. We just sat there watching the herd until it
.arted to move. There were enough men to handle it and
.made no move to follow.

"You're quiet," she said finally. "You don't say anything."

"What can I say?" I asked her honestly enough. "You've
.st said it all."

She didn't act mystified and want an explanation, for
.e knew as well as I what I meant and how I felt. She did
.ally say something, and it was so much what a lot of
.rls would have said that it enabled me to get my feet on

the ground again. She said, "You've only known me a fe~
hours."

"How long does it take? Is there a special time, ~
something? A special set of rules that says flatly a man h~
to know a girl three weeks, seventeen hours and nin~
minutes before he can fall in love with her? And anothe~
set that says she must know him six months, four hou~
and five minutes before she can admit she likes him?

"There isn't any time limit and there never has been~
I told her. "To some people it comes quick, to othe~
slow. With me it was the minute you walked out on th~
porch back there, and I rode into the yard. That's exactl~
when it was. The rest doesn't matter."

My voice wasn't a lover's voice. It was pretty sharp an~
hard because I felt just that way. Then it hit me all of ~
sudden and I could see it plain as day. "Well, at least h~
didn't steal you!"

She looked up quickly, her eyes going wide with su~
prise. "Steal me? Who?"

"Hugh Taylor," I said.

"Who?" She looked puzzled and a little frightene~
"What do you mean?"

"I mean Howie Taber—the one who was a friend ~
Lynch's, only his name is Hugh Taylor, and he's m~
cousin."

"Your cousin?" She was staring at me now, but the~
was not so much surprise in her eyes as I had expecte~
"What are you talking about?"

"I'm talking about a big blond and handsome man wi~
broad shoulders and deep-set blue eyes, a man with ~
small scar on the point of his chin, who rides good hors~
and wears flashy clothes and handles a gun well. That~
who I mean. A man who is my cousin but who could easi~
have called himself Howie Taber."

Her face was white now, but she was staring rig~
through me. "And what is your name?" she demanded.

"I'm Wat Bell," I told her. "I am the man Lynch w~
looking for at the Tin Cup, and how did he know I'd ~

ere? Only one man in all the world knew it, and that
n was Hugh—who I thought was my best friend."

"I don't believe that," she said. "I don't believe any of
You may know him, but you're an outlaw, masquerad-
; under a false name. You've made all this up."

"All right," I said, "I made it up!" With that I reined
horse around and started back for the T. If I had been
ing Rowdy I'd never have gone back at all, but this was
owhorse I'd borrowed, wanting to save the big black
er his long trek across country.

There was only one thing in my mind then, to get
wdy and hit the trail out of there, but fast. And where
Back to Texas! To prove that I hadn't killed my uncle.
prove that I was no outlaw.

The cowhorse I was on was a good horse and he took
over the hill to the T at a fast lope, and I came up from
hind the corrals and hit the dirt, and then stopped.
ght there across the yard from me was Ross Lynch, and
side him was Gene Bates. Win Dolliver was on the
p, and his face looked dark as death and just as solemn.
nch stepped out toward me and stopped. "Wat Bell!"
said. "I arrest you for murder!"

"Whose murder?" I demanded.

"The murder of Tom Ludlow!" he said. Then he smiled.
here is a charge against you in Texas, but we'll hang you
this one!"

I was mad all the way through. My hands swinging at
sides, I looked at him. "Ross Lynch, I did not murder
dlow, and you damn' well know it. You know it because
know who did! And I know! It was—!"

Gene Bates' hand swept down for a gun and so did
nch. My own guns were coming up and I took a quick
p forward and right and fired quickly—too quickly. My
t bullet knocked the gun from the sheriff's hand, and I
ln't intended it that way. I wanted to kill him. The
ond one took Gene Bates right over the belt buckle.

Win Dolliver hadn't moved. He stood there on the
ps, his eyes wide. But what he thought he wasn't

saying. I don't know where Maggie was. On the bur
house steps were two of the boys and another one stood
the corral. He turned to his saddle pockets and dug ou
box of .44s. "Catch!" he said simply, and tossed it.

"Thanks!" I caught the box in my left hand and back
toward the corral. Lynch was holding his numbed ha
and staring at me.

"I'll kill you for this!" he said. "I'll kill you if it's t
last thing I do!"

"If you do, it will be!" I told him. Astride the cowpor
I looked at Win. "Thanks, Dolliver. You've been migl
square. Tom Ludlow was killed by Gene Bates and I
Keys. That chip on the bone-handle of Keys' gun v
broken off when it fell into the rocks, you know where!

Then I reined my horse around and hit the trail a
fast run.

That pony had worked hard, but he was game. I
stayed with that run until he hit timber, and then I slow
him down to a canter, and then to a walk. After tha
began to Injun my trail. I took so many twists and turn
was dizzy, and I rode up and down several streams, acr
several shelves of rock and through some sand. And the
doubled back and headed for the Tin Cup.

My horse wouldn't go far and he needed rest. I need
food. There was food in the cabin, and every chance th
wouldn't think of it right away. Also, it was within striki
distance of the T, and I had no idea of leaving Row
That big black horse meant a lot to me, and ever since
Valverdes gave him to me, I'd treated him like a child.

Now I was an outlaw, having resisted arrest, the fi
crime I'd committed. But if I could prove that Bates a
Keys had killed Ludlow, and with the sheriff's knowled
I'd be in the clear even on that. And it was somethin
intended to prove.

From the expression on Lynch's face I knew that sho
ing of mine had been a distinct shock. Hugh hadn't warn

m about that simply because he didn't know. Hugh had
ays beaten me in shooting matches. That was before I
nt to Mexico. He had probably told Lynch I was only a
shot. Well, the shooting that knocked the gun from his
d and drilled Bates had been good shooting, the kind
wouldn't be too anxious to tackle again.

By sundown I was bedded down in the pines watching
Tin Cup ranchhouse. All through the final hours of
light I watched it and studied the trails. I wanted no
ps laid for me, although I doubted if they would think
he Tin Cup right away.

It was well after midnight before I started down the
l to the ranch, and I took my horse only a short
tance, then left him tied in the brush and cat-footed it
vn by myself, leaving my spurs on the horn of my
dle.

Nothing looked very good right then. I had killed
ne Bates and resisted arrest. Hugh Taylor, whom I'd
sidered my best friend, had tried to trap me into an
bush, and Maggie Dolliver, the girl I wanted more
n anything in life, was in love with Hugh. Right then
about as little to live for as any man, but I'd a lot of
entment—nor was I one to bow my head before the
rm and ride off letting well enough alone.

When I did ride off it would be with my name clear,
also I would know and the world would know who had
ed Uncle Tom Bell. Until then I had a job to do.

The warm sun of the late afternoon had baked the
und hard after the rain, and I moved carefully. The
e house was dark and still when I tried the door, and
ased open without a sound. Once inside I wasted no
e, for while Win had been making coffee on the day of
killing, I had seen where the food was kept. Hastily, I
hed for the coffee sack. It was almost empty!

Puzzled, for it had been nearly full when I last saw it, I
hed for the beans, and they were gone. And then
re was a whisper of movement behind me and I turned,
ning my gun as I moved.

"Don't shoot!" The voice was low, but the very sou
of it thrilled me so that I couldn't have squeezed a trig
if I'd wished. "The food is on the table, all packed."

"Mag! You did this . . . for me?" I couldn't beli
that, and moved around the table toward her. She l
been in that inner room, waiting behind the blank
covered door.

"Yes." The word was simple and honest. "I did it
you, and I've no idea whether I'm doing right or n
Maybe all they say about you is true. Maybe you did
your uncle and maybe you did kill Tom Ludlow."

"You don't believe that?"

"No." She hesitated. "No, I don't believe I do. I kn
Ross Lynch, Wat—that is your name, isn't it? He has b
mixed up in so many wrong things. It was the only fau
could find with Howie—that he trailed with Lynch a
that devil, Bill Keys."

In the darkness I could not see her eyes, but sudde
my hands lifted to her shoulders. "Mag," I said sof
"I've got to ride out of here. Whatever else I do, I've
to clear myself, and I'm going to do it, an' if the trou
strays over on somebody else's range, I'm going to foll
it there.

"I could go away now, taking the blame for Old N
Ludlow like they've already hung the blame on me
Uncle Tom, but I won't do it. I won't have you doubt
me, even if I never see you again. Nor do I want folks
think I've killed Uncle Tom, after he did so much for me

She didn't say anything for a moment, and with l
arms all warm under my hands it was all I could do
keep from drawing her close. Finally, she spoke. "
what you have to do, Wat. I know how you feel."

"But, Mag, suppose that somebody you— Well, I me
suppose that when I find who did this killing, I find it
somebody close to you. What then?"

She looked up at me again. "Why, then, Wat, it wo
have to be that way. I guess I knew you felt like this
knew who you believed was guilty, but I came here a

t this food ready for you, sure that you'd come. I brought
ur horse, too, Wat. He's in the shadow by the stable."

"Rowdy?" My voice lifted, then lowered. "You did
t? Oh, you darlin'! Now I'll feel like a man again! This
ny, he tries hard and he's got a great heart, but he's not
wdy."

"I knew how you felt about him." She drew back.
ow you'd better go. Ride out of here, and good luck,
atever you do, or whatever comes!"

napter IV
rsethief Valley

at was just the way I left, with that pack over my
ulder, slipping out to find Rowdy, who nudged me
th his nose and stamped contentedly. But I waited there
til she was on her horse and gone, and then I slid into
e saddle and headed for the hills. When I got to where
left the pony, I tied the bridle reins up and turned him
se, knowing he'd find his way back to the T.

Already I'd had an idea. Bill Keys had come from the
adshaws, and that was where I was heading, right for
rsethief Valley. There had to be a tie-up there. Nor was
vaiting until morning. Rowdy was rested and ready for
e trail, and I took it, riding west across the mountains,
rting Latigo, and heading on west. On the third night I
nped at Badger Spring, up a creek from the canyon of
e Agua Fria, and after a quick breakfast in the morning,
ssed the Bumblebee and Black Canyon and headed up
e Dead Cow. Skirting the peak on a bench I cut down
e mountainside into Horsethief Canyon.

Western men knew the West, and it was no wonder
at even as far east as Dimmit County, Texas, we knew
ut the horsethief trails that cut through the country
m Robber's Roost and the Hole in the Wall to Mexico.
is place was only a way station, but from all I'd heard I

knew some of the crowd that trailed stolen horses, a
they were a hard bunch of men.

Rowdy had a feeling for trouble. The big black prick
his ears toward the ramshackle cluster of cabins and c
rals that lay on the flat among the mountains. Nobo
needed to tell me that we were not watched all the w
down that trail, and when Rowdy drew up in front of t
combination saloon and store that was the headquarters
Horsethief, a half-dozen men idled on the steps.

Across at the big barn a man sat on a bench with
Henry rifle across his knees, and another man whittl
idly in front of a cabin even further along.

When I swung down I tied Rowdy to the rail a
stepped up on the porch and dug out the making
"Howdy," I offered.

A lean, hatchet-faced man, who looked the type
murder his mother-in-law, looked up. "Howdy."

Nobody said anything and when I'd built a smoke
offered the tobacco around, but nobody made a move
accept. A short, stocky rider with run-down heels on
boots squatted against the wall. He looked up at me, th
nodded at Rowdy. "Quite a hoss. Looks like he cou
make miles.'"

"He made 'em to here." I looked at Shorty aga
"Want a drink? I'll buy."

He got up with alacrity. "Never refused a drink!"
warned me. We pushed through the doors and bellied
to the bar. There was a smell of cured bacon, dry good
and spices curiously intermingled. I glanced around t
store, and sized up the fat man in the dirty shirt w
bounced around to the bar side and made a casual swipe
the bar top with a rag.

"What'll it be, gents?"

Shorty chuckled. "He says 'what'll it be' ever'time, a
he ain't had nothing but Injun whiskey over this bar in
year!"

Fatty was indignant. "Injun whiskey, my eye!" he e
ploded. "This here's my own make, an' mighty good r

kker if I do say so! Injun whiskey!" he snorted. "You've
een drinkin' out of horse tracks an' buffalo wallers so long
ou don't know a good drink when you get one!"

He placed two glasses on the bar and a bottle. Shorty
oured for them both, but Fatty reached for the bottle as
e put it down. "Leave the bottle," I told him, "we'll want
nother." I placed a gold piece on the bar, and Fatty
icked it up so fast it looked like a wink of light.

"Better not flash that coin around if you've got more of
:," Shorty warned. "Especially when Wolf Kettle is around.
Ie's the hombre you talked to out yonder, an' while Davis
s away, he's ramroddin' the outfit."

"Things look kind of slow," I suggested.

"They sure are!" Shorty's disgust was evident. "Noth-
ng doing at all! From what we hear there's to be some-
hing big movin' soon, but you can't tell. Where you
:om?"

"Down Sonora way. They call me the Papago Kid."

"Shorty Carver's my handle." He looked up at me.
Sonora, is it? Well, I sure figured I knew you." He spoke
oftly all of a sudden. "I'd of sworn you were an hombre I
aw sling a gun up to Dodge, one time. An hombre name
f Wat Bell, from a Texas outfit."

"If you think I look like him," I suggested, "forget it.
Ie might not like the resemblance!"

Shorty laughed. "Sure thing! You can be anybody you
vant with me. What's on your mind? You wantin' to join
p?"

"Not exactly. I'm huntin' a couple of friends of mine.
3ill Keys and an hombre named Taber."

Shorty Carver's face hardened. "You won't find 'em
ere, an' if they are friends of yours, sure you'd better
unt another sidekick than me. That Taber an' I didn't get
long."

I took a sidelong look at Shorty. "He's been here
hen?"

"Been here?" Shorty looked around at me. "He was
ere yesterday!"

"*What?*"

My question was so sharp that a half-dozen head turned our way, and I lowered my voice. "Did yo say—*yesterday?*"

"Sure did! He rode in here about sunup, an' him ar Davis had a long confab. Then Davis takes off for Sku Valley, and where Taber went, I don't know. He rode ou of here, headin' east."

For several minutes I didn't say a word. If Hugh wa out here, that meant the time for a showdown had come Yet what had I found? Nothing to date that would help That Hugh Taylor had been known to the outlaws c Horsethief Canyon was something, but not much.

Right then I began to wonder for the first time abou those absences from the ranch when Hugh was growin up. And that time he had returned with that silver-mounte saddle and a good bit of money. It was becoming mor apparent where that money had come from. Had Uncl Tom Bell guessed? He was a sharp old man, and had no ridden the trails and plains for nothing. He could rea sign wherever it was . . . and here was another though perhaps he had read the truth and guessed at what la behind those absences and jumped Hugh about it.

Had Hugh killed his uncle?

There was enough of the old feeling for Hugh left t make me revolt at the idea, and yet it began to seem mor and more possible. Uncle Tom and I had a violent quarre and I left. What would be easier than to kill him and le me take the blame? Hugh's surprise at my sudden retur could have come from his consternation at what it migh mean to him, and also he might have believed thos rumors that I had been killed in Mexico.

Certainly, he managed to get me out of the countr without seeing anyone else.

The swinging doors shoved wide and Kettle came in He took a sidelong glance at me and walked up to the ba at my side and ordered a drink. I could smell trouble com ing and could see there was something in Kettle's craw.

He got his drink and turned to me. "We don't wel-
me strangers here!" he said. "State your business, an'
le on out!"

That turned me around, but I took my time. The man
ritated me, and I didn't feel like side-stepping trouble. I
as tired of running and ready for a showdown, and ready
back it with lead. "Kettle," I said clearly, "I didn't come
here to see you. I never heard of you. You may run a
g herd where you come from, but where I ride that herd
oks like mighty small gathering!"

His face darkened a little, and the yellow lights in his
es were plainer. He half-turned before I spoke, but I
ve it to him fast. "Don't try to run any blazers on
e, Kettle, because they won't stick. If you make rough
lk with me, it's gun talk, and if you draw on me, I'll
ll you!"

Shorty Carver had stepped wide of me and was stand-
g there facing the room. What his play would be, I
uldn't know. He was a friend of only a few minutes, yet
ere had been some spark of comradeship there such as
e often finds with men of the same ilk and the same
ckground. He spoke before either of us could make a
ove. "He came to see Taber and Keys," Shorty warned,
hey sent for him!"

"What?" Carver's statement obviously stopped Kettle.
Iow do you know that?"

"Because I told him," I said simply.

He glared at me suspiciously. Something was gnawing
the man, and it might be something about me, but I
d the feeling that he was naturally mean, a trouble
inter, a man with a burr under his saddle. "Where'd you
ow Taber?" he demanded.

"In Texas," I said calmly, "and I knew Bill Keys in
nora." That last was sheer hope, for whether Keys had
er been below the Border, I didn't know.

"He's the Papago Kid," Carver said.

"Never heard of him!" Kettle returned sharply.

Another man spoke up, a lean-faced man with a droop-

ing black mustache. "I have," he said. "He's the homb
that killed Albie Dick."

Kettle's eyes sharpened, and I knew that meant som
thing to this man. Albie Dick had been a dangerous ma
and a killer with fifteen dead men on his trail when v
tangled in Sonora.

"That's neither here nor there," I said calmly. "I wa
to talk to Howie Taber!"

"You'll have to wait," Kettle said grudgingly. "He ai
here."

Somehow, the men relaxed. Shorty returned to the b
and took another drink. Under his breath, he warne
"You'd better watch yourself. Wolf was never braced li
that before. He'll be careful to make his play at the rig
time, but you've got trouble. The man's mean as a rattler

He downed his drink. "Also," he added, "I'm begi
ning to remember things. That Wat Bell who downed th
man in Abilene was ramrodding an XY herd . . . and tha
the ranch we're going to use in Texas!"

"What do you mean? Going to use?"

He looked at me quickly, sharply. "So? You dor
know the inside on this, do you?" He was silent, traci
circles on the bar with the bottom of his glass. "Just wh
is between you and Taber, Kid?"

That was a sticker, and I hesitated. Shorty had sa
earlier that he had no use for Taber. Right then I knew n
time here was short, and a friend would be a help. A
other enemy would be little worse. "Taber's my cousin,"
said frankly, speaking low. "I think he killed my uncle ar
framed me with the murder while I was in Mexico. Fu
thermore, I think he sent me out here to lay low ar
planned to have me murdered when I arrived."

Quietly, I explained in as few words as possible ar
from time to time he nodded. "Glad you told me," I
said. "Also there's no posters on Wat Bell out here, so yc
must be right on figuring that Lynch was out to get you

"No posters on me? How do you know that?"

He grinned, and he said softly. "Because I'm a Catt

sociation detective, pardner, an' I'm studyin' into the
ggest steal of horses an' cattle ever organized!"

Together we walked outside, and the story he told me
swered a lot of questions. For several years a steady
eam of stolen stock had been sent south over the old
rsethief trail from the Hole in the Wall and Robber's
oost to Mexico, and this valley was one of the important
y stations. Lately, it had become apparent that even
ger things were in the wind, for a man lately associated
th the gang had suddenly become owner of a Panhandle
nch in Texas. There was a reported tie-up with the XY
central southern Texas, and large quantities of stock had
gun to disappear and move south toward the Border. It
d begun to look as if mass stealings of stock had begun,
oving south under cover and with large ranches as way
tions.

"Who's behind it?" I asked him. "Any guesses on
at?"

"Uh huh. There is." Shorty Carver lit a smoke. "Howie
ber's behind it. That cousin of yours has turned out to
the brains of the biggest stock-stealing ring in the
untry."

From the time he was sixteen until he was twenty,
gh Taylor had been absent from the XY. He had gone
ain shortly after, and obviously, he had been gone at
st once during the time I was in Mexico. It was then,
doubt, that he had begun to round up old cronies of his
rlier days and build the ring that Carver now told me
out.

"Shorty," I said, "can you slip out of here?"

"Uh huh."

"Then wire the sheriff in Dimmit County. See if I'm
lly wanted there for murder. Also, check on Tom Bell's
ll, see who that XY spread was left to when he died. I'm
ving a talk with that cousin of mine!" I hesitated, think-
g. "See you at the Tin Cup!"

"Watch your step!" Shorty warned. "Hugh isn't so bad,
t you watch Bill Keys and Kettle!"

Chapter V
Power of the Papago Kid

After he was gone, I idled around, getting the lay of t]
land and thinking things over. It was well along in t]
afternoon, and night soon to come. By this time Hu]
would know that I was still alive, that the plot to get r]
at the Tin Cup had failed. Evidently, the Tin Cup h]
been chosen because of its secluded position, and Lyn]
and Keys had been informed by the friend where I h]
stopped last that I was coming. Accordingly, they h]
evidently waited. It might be that I had been spott]
and reported at several places since then, and they h]
come out to meet me, either at the Tin Cup or on the tr]
near there.

Probably they had managed to get Ludlow away fro]
his ranch, or had reason to believe he would be awa]
Then they had either killed him by mistake, or had kill]
him because he returned too soon. No doubt they h]
plans for the Tin Cup, anyway, as the ranch was ideal f]
such a venture as they planned.

The jumpiness was in me now that presaged danger]
could sense it all around me, and I was restless. Eve]
man here would be an enemy once it was realized who]
was, and at any moment Bill Keys, Hugh Taylor, or Ro]
Lynch might ride in, and then the lid would blow off.]
was surrounded by unfriendly guns, and to blast my w]
out would be a forlorn hope.

Mingled with the realization of my danger was]
acute longing to be back with Maggie Dolliver. No wom]
had ever affected me as she had, and despite the fact th]
there was an understanding between herself and Hugh,]
had the feeling that she had felt for me as I had for he]
That she had brought Rowdy to me and packed the fo]
was enough to show that she believed in me.

Time and again I walked down to the corral to talk]
Rowdy. Time and again I noted exactly where my sadd]

, and calculated every move it would take to resaddle
. That was something I wanted to do, but not until it
dark. To saddle him now would serve only as a warn-
of impending departure. I wanted them to believe that
as content to await the return of the man they knew as
wie Taber.

Yet I could feel the suspicion, and my own restlessness
tributed to it. Wolf watched me sharply, his yellowish
s rarely leaving me. Other men seemed always around,
apparently Shorty Carver had managed to slip away.
ce he was accepted here, his going and coming would
asion little remark.

My thoughts kept reverting to Maggie and Win. At
Win was my friend, and it was something to have
n one friend now. Once more I returned to the saloon
seated myself in a chair against the wall, careful to
p my guns clear. Evening was coming, and the sun had
ped down behind Wasson Peak and the ridges around
All the bright glare of the Arizona sun was gone, and
desert and mountains had turned to soft pastel shades.
lue quail called out in the brush, and somewhere a
ro yawned his lonely call into the cool air of twilight. A
r slammed, and then I heard water splashing as some-
dipped a bucket into the spring. There was a subdued
rmur of voices, and the rattle of dishes. There was no
ger in me, only that poised alertness that kept my eyes
ving and my every muscle and nerve aware and ready.

Casually I arose to my feet and stretched. Then, as I
a dozen times before, I sauntered carelessly down to
corral. Wolf Kettle watched me, but I ignored him,
pping near the corrals to look around. Then I stepped
r and put my hand on Rowdy's neck and spoke to him.
r a minute I crawled through the poles and was out of
t of Wolf or any of the others.

My movements were swift and sure. Rowdy was never
led or saddled faster in his life, and in what seemed
cely no time, I was sauntering back into sight, crawl-
once more through the corral bar. I slowly rolled a

smoke, struck a match, and then ambled placidly a
nonchalantly back toward the store. "Brother," I told r
self, "if you get out of here with a whole skin, you
lucky."

Back in my chair I listened to the casual talk, scarc
paying attention until suddenly two horses rounded i
sight. They were walking, and they came so suddenly t
it was a surprise to all of us. They came from the ot
side of the saloon and stopped at the end of the po
opposite me.

Two men swung down. "Wolf? You got some g
ready?"

It was Hugh Taylor!

My heart pounding, I slowly lowered my hands to
knees, my eyes riveted on him.

"You'd better have!" The second man was speaki
and it was Bill Keys. "I'm hungry as a grizzly!"

It was late dusk, and no faces could be distinguish
Hugh came up on the porch, looking tall, strong, a
familiar. Suddenly it was hard to think of him as being
outlaw, an enemy. I could only recall the times we w
swimming together, the horses we swapped, and the tir
we played hooky from school and went hunting.

He happened to turn his head then, and he loo
right at me. He could have seen no more than a bl
figure of a man, seated there, but there must have b
something familiar about it. "Who's that?" His voice r
sharply.

"It's me, Hugh!" I said softly, "I figured it was ab
time we had a little talk."

At my voice Keys jerked like he'd been struck, and
turned. Wolf was facing me too. The three of them ring
around me, from my extreme left to full front. On
right side, the edge of the porch, there was no one.

"You . . . ? Wat?" There was an edge of something
his voice, doubt, uncertainty or something. Maybe he v
remembering, too. "We've nothing to talk about, noth
at all."

"What about Uncle Tom, Hugh? I didn't kill him. . . .
d you?"

His breath drew sharply. "We won't talk about that,
at. Not right now. You shouldn't have come here, you
ow that."

"Do I, Hugh? You sent me to the Tin Cup, didn't you?
as I supposed to be killed there? Did you figure to send
ur own cousin, who grew up with you, to get killed?"

I knew Western men. Even the outlaws were rarely
el men. Many of them were punchers who had rustled
e wrong stock once too often, some of them were men
o had been too handy with a gun, but few of them were
lly bad men. Rather they were often reckless and care-
s in a land where many men were reckless and where
operty rights were uncertain. Among them were, of
urse, killers and men of criminal instincts, yet I was
ying for those others.

He didn't answer me, so I went on talking, not raising
voice, just an easy conversational tone, yet all the time
ery nerve was on edge.

"They killed the wrong man, Hugh, and now I'm
king into things. I've been asking questions—about
cle Tom's will, and whether I'm really wanted for
rder or not, and now I'm getting mighty curious about
."

"You're too curious." His mind seemed to be made up,
d I sensed an almost regretful note. "You should never
ve come back from Mexico, Wat. You messed up every-
ng when you did that. You should have stayed down
re. Now you're into something that's too big for you.
u're playing with company that's too fast."

"Am I?" I laughed, although there was no humor in it.
o, I'm not, Hugh. You've just continued to think of me
your kid cousin. I've covered a lot of country since
n, and traveled in faster company than you'll ever
ow."

"That's right, Boss." It was the man with the black
stache again. "This hombre is the Papago Kid. He

rubbed out Albie Dick an' led the roundup of his outf
Nobody got away."

"So the kid's grown up!" There was an edge of sarcas
in Hugh's voice. "That makes it a little better. I'd not li
to be responsible for anybody taking advantage of you."

"You've still got a chance, Hugh," I said quietly. "Y
can break this up right now. Turn the killers of Ludl
over to the law, confess your part in this plot, and lea
the country."

"Are you crazy?" He was genuinely angry now. "Yo
Giving *me* a chance!"

"Then your answer is no?" I could see that Bill Ke
and Kettle were growing restive. For their taste we h
talked too long, and neither of them liked the tone of it

"You fool!" Contempt was thick in his voice. "Y
should never have come back from Mexico! Worse, y
should have never come here! You should have hightail
it out of the country! I don't want to kill you, but ther
no choice!"

There was one more thing. Nor could I resist it. "H
could I leave, Hugh? I fell in love with Maggie!"

"*What?*" He wheeled so quickly to face toward n
again that he gave me the one big break I'd needed.
went off that porch in one jump and ducked around t
corner of the house. I'd never have dared chance it w
Keys and Kettle having their eyes on me, but when Hu
turned he partially blocked them off. I hit the grou
running and skidded into the shadow of a clump of m
quite. Then I gave out with a piercing whistle.

One shot cut the brush in reply to my whistle, but t
whistle stopped them. They didn't know what it meant.
seemed like a signal and they were immediately afrai
had help nearby. It was a signal, but not for help. It v
for Rowdy.

He knew what to do. On that signal he would un
himself if tied with a slip knot, or nose down cor
bars. It was a trick I'd taught him, along with a doz
others.

The rattle of hooves sounded, and I heard somebody
. "The corral's open! Somebody's there!"

I whistled again, and the big black horse wheeled
ween the buildings. Somebody cracked down on me
in, and that time I had enough of being the target in a
oting gallery. I glimpsed a dark form and let fly, and
rd a grunt, and the sound of something falling, and
n I was in the saddle and taking out across the valley.

My route was in my mind. I'd gotten it from Shorty,
knew the area. Rowdy took off down Horsethief Can-
at a dead run, then slowed and turned sharply left up
ail to the bench. We had the mountain for a back-
und and were lost in the blackness there, and Rowdy
ld walk like a cat when the chips were down. We
ssed the shoulder of the mountain south of the ranch
hit the head of Sycamore, and down Sycamore to the
l that ran south, running parallel to Black Canyon.
n I crossed the table to the Agua Fria again, and took
up Squaw Creek.

The advantage of darkness and the best horse was
e, and I used it. Danger would come with morning,
I was hoping that Shorty would meet me at the
nbling T with news that was good. Whatever else
pened, I would see Maggie once more, and it was
th the ride and worth the danger.

Morning lifted the darkness away and brought back the
-bright hills to view. I liked the feel of the country and
air on my face, and the feel of a good horse between
knees. Behind me was the end of something, the end
ll the old days when I was a kid on the XY, of Uncle
n Bell, crabby and lovable, but honest as the day—and
gh, older than I, and skillful in all things. We'd never
n close, and yet we'd done a lot together, as boys will,
I we had grown older together. It is a sad thing to leave
iend behind, to find one you've admired changed.

When the sun was high I turned into a deep arroyo

and found a wide shadow where I could swing down a
strip the saddle from Rowdy. After I'd cared for him
picketed him on a little grass, then slept for an hour. Af
I'd eaten, I saddled up again. The sun had bridged
space that divides morning from afternoon and, still bl
ing hot, had turned just a little toward the west whe
started on. Altogether I'd spent nearly three hours in t
arroyo.

The sun reflected from a distant flat rock, and t
clouds left shadows on the desert floor. I studied the
reach of the valley and then kept to the low grou
moving in shadows of clouds and up washes and where t
ground was broken, yet I saw no one. We were headed
a showdown, Rowdy and I, but it would be at the T,
maybe the Tin Cup. It would not be here.

The Tin Cup lay chill and quiet in the moonlight wh
Rowdy walked down the trail. We drew up, looking t
place over, and it was still as death. The comparison ca
into my mind and made me shiver a little. That v
striking too close to the truth.

Skirting the place warily, I seemed to detect a dar
spot among the pines, and circled toward it. Then I dr
up and listened. I heard a horse stamp and blow, th
stillness. Speaking to Rowdy so he would not whinny
moved in.

A lone man was camped in the pines near a strea
Watching, I heard a light footfall, then turned. Sho
Carver was standing there on the edge of the bru
"Rolled my bed up an' laid out in the brush, myse
he said. "Figured it some safer. They might get wary
me."

He held out two wires, and shielding the flame w
my hat, I struck a match and read them.

DISCHARGED MEXICAN HAND CONFESSED SLAYING O
BELL. NO ONE WANTED HERE.

A distinct feeling of relief hit me, just as much for ⌐gh as for myself. If he had taken advantage of my ⌐sence to claim the ranch all for himself, I could not have ⌐med him, but if he had killed Uncle Tom . . . I ripped ⌐en the other message.

TOM BELL'S WILL LEAVES XY TO WAT BELL WHEN HE RE-
TURNS. BELL'S REASON WAS 'HE STAYED WITH ME AND
HELPED TO BUILD IT.' IN EVENT OF BELL'S NOT RETURN-
ING, RANCH TO GO TO HUGH TAYLOR.

So, then I was not a fugitive, but owner of two hun-
⌐ed thousand acres of rangeland and a huge herd of
⌐ttle. Somehow, I couldn't find it in me to blame Hugh
⌐ much. Probably he had believed me killed in Mexico,
⌐d that he was the owner of the XY.

This crooked business was another thing. Uncle Tom
⌐uld turn over in his grave if he thought the old XY was
⌐ing used as a clearing ground or holding ground for
⌐stled stock.

"We're heading for the T," I told Carver, "you've seen
⌐ese messages?"

"Read 'em when they came in," he said. "Taylor tried
⌐ have you ambushed here. That isn't a theory anymore.
⌐e've got Ross Lynch."

"Got him? Arrested?"

"Yeah, last night. There was hell to pay in Latigo. We
⌐nd Ross in the hills with some rustled stock, an' he ran
⌐ it. We got him in Latigo. He confessed on his deathbed."

⌐hapter VI
⌐e Hard Way Out

⌐ght then I knew we were in the wrong place. If Ross
⌐nch had been shot down and confessed, by this time
⌐gh would know it. So would Keys and Kettle!

In that event they would know their game was up, an that within a matter of hours they would have poss closing down on them from all sides. Which meant th Hugh Taylor would be riding to the Tumbling T!

Or would he?

"Let's ride!" I said sharply. "He'll head for the T to s Mag, or I'm off my head! Or maybe to see me for showdown. In any event, Keys and Kettle will want to s me, an' from what I told them at Horsethief Canyo they'll know where to come! Let's go!"

Not waiting for Shorty to saddle, I threw a leg ov Rowdy and lit out over the trail to the Tumbling T. Th ride was one of the fastest I ever made on a horse, an Rowdy felt like running. We took off down the trail an skirted the cliffs until I could see the moonlight on th roofs at the T. The whole place was ablaze with lights, so slowed down. Leaving Rowdy in the shadow of the stor stable, I moved up toward the house.

It was almost daylight, and the sky was growing gra In the ranch yard were several horses, and I could see dark group of them standing beyond the house, and se eral men were loitering about. Whoever was here was o the ground in force. On cat feet, I Injuned up to th house and slid in close to a window. Inside were sever people. I could see Win Dolliver, his face dark and angr and with him was Maggie. She was as pale as he was dar and her eyes were wide.

"He's not here and he hasn't been here in days Maggie was saying. "Now take your men and get out!"

"He'll come here!" That was Keys speaking. "He gone soft on you. He told Hugh he was in love with you

Her eyes went to Hugh. "He said that?" Her ch lifted. "Well, all right, then! I'm in love with him!"

My heart jumped and I gripped the windowsill har Yet Hugh was speaking now, and I listened. "So? You so me out, did you? You dropped me for another man?"

She turned to him. "I'm sorry, Hugh. I was intendir to tell you. I was never in love with you, and you know i

ed you, yes. You persuaded me and I listened, but I
er felt sure about you, never liked the company you
:." Bill Keys laughed harshly at that. "And I hoped
d change. You didn't.

'Then he came along, and from then on I knew there
d never be anyone else."

'He beats me out of my ranch and out of my girl!"
;h said bitterly. "That's a pretty thing!"

'I think you tried to rob him, Hugh," Maggie said,
l you tried to have him murdered!"

'I wish I had!" he complained bitterly.

'Boss," Keys interrupted, "let's get outside an' get the
; set. If he's comin', he'll be here soon."

'Hugh," Maggie warned, "if you don't take your men
leave here at once, I'll hate you!"

'Wouldn't that be awful!" Keys sneered.

Hugh Taylor turned on him. "Be still!" he said sharply.
make the comments here!"

Keys' eyes narrowed angrily. "You'd better make 'em,
!" he snapped. "You've sure played hell with all your
y figurin'! Mixin' this fancy doll into this has messed it
or sure! Take the boys an' light out of here! I'll take
of Mister Wat Bell when he comes!"

'You'd better get outside and wait until I come!" Hugh
sharply. "I don't want any comments made about
; Dolliver!"

Bill Keys stared at Hugh, his eyes ugly with hatred.
n't get high an' mighty, Taber, or whatever your name
We follered you because you figured things right and
made money. This deal looked good until you got to
n' women with it, but don't think we can't get shut of
just as quick if we decide we want to!"

Hugh Taylor turned on Keys. "Are you huntin' a show-
n?" he demanded.

That was my cue to get away from that window. In
e long, silent jumps I made it to the back door and
d inside. I took it easy, and no more than a word or
could have passed before I was just inside the kitchen

and could hear them in the next room. Keys was on
prod, I could see that.

"Showdown?" Keys was saying. "I reckon there woul[
be no showdown betwixt you an' me, Taber. If we're g
to kill Wat Bell we'd better get outside. We can settle
later, but I'm tellin' you, don't go to givin' me orders!
in that voice!"

Hugh's voice was icy. "All right, Keys! Let's go outsi

I knew that tone! I'd heard it before, and this w
showdown whether Keys wanted it or not. He had rid
some rough trails since I'd known him, Hugh had, b
doubted that he was gun-slick enough to stack up rigł
a gun scrap with either Keys or Kettle.

Keys and Kettle went outside, and Hugh follo
them. In a quick step I was into the room. Win wheele
the sound of my movement, and Mag stood riveted wl
she was. "Wat! Oh, you mustn't be found here! Go aw.

"Win, you take care of her!" She had come right to
arms, and I was holding her close, looking over my sh
der at Dolliver. "Get a shotgun—you've got one, I kı
Get all your shells. If the worst comes to the worst, si
them off with that. I'm going out there!"

"You're a fool to do that, Wat!" Win said seriou
"You won't have a chance, man!"

"No, I've got to side Hugh. They are going to kill I
He can't see it, either. He can't see that Keys wan
showdown. They've got the idea from him, most of
work and planning is done, so now Keys an' Kettle fi
it's all over. They want to get rid of him."

"You'd side the man who tried to have you kille
Win was incredulous.

I shrugged, knowing I was probably a fool. "He's
cousin. We grew up like brothers, and Uncle Tom we
have liked it that way. Anyway, those men out there
my enemies as well as his."

From the door I took a quick, careful look at the y
This was it, all right. Keys had walked a dozen feet a
from Hugh and turned to face him. Wolf Kettle had stro

to the right, at least fifty feet from Keys. They made
corners with Hugh Taylor as the point of the triangle.
Keys spoke first. "Taber, we don't like this setup. We
't like you lordin' it over us an' comin' the high an'
hty around. We don't like you takin' most of the money,
er. We've decided to cut you out of the deal."

Maybe I'm coldblooded, but I was curious. I wanted to
how much of the Bell blood there was in Hugh. For
first time in his life, so far as I knew, Hugh was called
to face, and if ever a man was called by a pair of curly
ves from the way back and rough, it was these two.
at would he do? That was what I wondered.

For almost a half minute he didn't say anything, but he
t have been thinking plenty, and when he spoke, I
ld have cheered. The hombre may have tried to frame
he may have hit the wrong trails, but he was my
sin. "Why, sure, Bill!" he said. "You do want a show-
n, don't you? And you, Kettle? Sure there's more of
coyote in you than the wolf. This is what they called
ng a man the Black Spot in a story I read once. Funny
g, it was a pirate story, and I read it with Wat—a
er man than either of you!"

He took a step further toward them, his eyes shifting
n one to the other. "Spread wide, aren't you? Well, I'll
 one of you to hell with me, anyway!"

Their hands were poised when I stepped out of the
r. As I stepped out, I spoke. "Which one do you want,
gh? I'll take the other! I'm siding you!"

Keys' eyes lifted to me, then Kettle's. They weren't
py about this change in the situation, not even a little
 Hugh did not turn a hair. "Take Kettle," he said,
ys has been begging for it!"

"There's a good bit of skunk in both of them," I said
lly. "Trot out your coyote, Kettle! You asked for it!" I
 the ground with a jump, digging in both heels and
ving as I landed.

Kettle flashed a fast gun, I'll say that for him, and he
ped into a crouch snarling like the Wolf he was named

for. I saw his gun wink red, and then I was walking
him, triggering my right-hand Colt.

Kettle fired and fired again, and then my second
hit him just below the shirt pocket and he lifted up on
tiptoes and I slammed another one in for good measu
He went down, clawing at the dirt with both hands,
then I turned on my heel to see Hugh was down on
face, but struggling to get up, and Keys was cursing
ciously and trying to get a gun up for one more shot.

"Drop it, Bill!" I yelled. "Drop it or take it!"

The face he turned on me was a mask of viciousne
Down he might be, and badly wounded, but he wa
cornered cougar at that moment, boiling with all his
nate viciousness. His gun came up, and I felt the shoc
the bullet, then the report. I got my balance and lifted
gun, then fired. The shot turned him around on his kn
and dropped him, but he wouldn't die.

With a lunge, he got to his feet. His shirt was soa
with blood and he stood there tottering and opened up
me with both guns. They turned into coughing, spitt
flame, and I took another step straight forward and fi
again, then shifted guns and slammed two more into h

Still snarling, he took a step back, so full of lead he
top-heavy, but he stood there, cursing wickedly and g
ing at me. Then his eyes seemed to glaze over,
mouthing curses, he went to the ground. I turned
took a look back at Kettle, but he was done for.

Looking up at the dark line of men near the horse
told them, "This is it, boys! Drop your guns!"

They must have thought me completely crazy. I
hit once and maybe more, and my guns were aln
empty, yet I was calling twelve hard-case riders, al
them gun handlers.

"That's right!" It was Shorty Carver from the ba
"Let go your belts easy! We've got you covered!"

"I'm holding a shotgun, and there's plenty of shel
Win chimed in from the house.

They hesitated, and I didn't blame them. There we

zen of them, but they could see the rifle from the barn,
d the shotgun from the house. The rifle was a Spencer,
ing a .56 caliber bullet of 360 grains. It took no great
agination to realize that while some of them might, and
bably would, get away, the Spencer would account for
veral, and a man hit with a .56 caliber bullet doesn't
vel far. As for the shotgun, it had twin barrels, and that
ant two dead men without reloading. As for me, I was
tering on my feet, but I'd missed only one shot of all I'd
ed, and nobody wanted to gamble I'd miss more. It was
cinch anywhere from four to seven of them would hit
t before the rest got away. And nobody was sure he
uldn't be one of the seven.

"To hell with it!" The black-mustached man who had
alled me from Sonora let go his belts, and it was a
nal. They all did likewise.

At that moment a half-dozen riders swept down the
l and into the yard. Two of them wore badges. I turned
l walked slowly toward Hugh as Win and Maggie rushed
m the house toward me.

Dropping on one knee, I turned Hugh over gently.
s eyes flickered open, and he looked at me. There was
thing anybody could do for him. Bill Keys hadn't been
ssing any shots, and the only wonder was that Hugh
s still alive.

"Thanks, kid!" he whispered. "You were right on time!
u an' Mag . . . I'm glad! Real glad!" His breath sobbed
his lungs for three deep, agonized gasps, and then he
ke again. "Unc . . . le Tom . . . he told me why . . .
t ranch . . . you. Knew I was . . . crook. . . . I was a
l."

We got him inside then, and along about three that
rning, he hung up his spurs.

In another room, I was having my own trouble, for I'd
en two slugs instead of one, and the Doc had to dig one
hem out. It came hard, but I had a bullet to bite on while
probed for it. Mag was with me, with me all the time,
ough twice I sent her to see how Hugh was coming.

He came out of it, Hugh did, just before the end, a[nd] when he did, I got out of bed and went in. Doc told m[e] was crazy, but I went.

He looked up at me from the bed. "It's all squa[re,] Hugh," I said. "Tell Uncle Tom hello."

"You think I'll see him?" he asked me, and his vo[ice] was mighty hoarse.

"Sure you will!" I said. "Any cowhand might take [a] wrong trail once, or put the wrong brand on a cow! I thi[nk] the Inspector up there can read your brand right!"

"Thanks, kid," he said. "When you grew up, you s[ure] grew tall!"

I took his hand then, and he was looking up at [me] when his eyes blinked and his grip tightened, then lo[os]ened. "He's all yours, boy," I said softly. "Let him ha[ve] his head!"

You know, I'll swear he smiled. . . . It was really som[e]thing, after all, to have a friend like Hugh.

The
Sixth Shotgun

Author's Note

ot of people in the early days of the West did not
eve in courts. They preferred to judge a culprit and
cute the sentence right on the spot.

For many, it was a simple matter of expediency. Sup-
e you caught a man branding one of your cattle out in
field. Putting a gun on him, you took him into town,
ch may have been fifty miles away, to turn him over to
sheriff. You then rode back to your ranch.

In a few days you had to ride all the way back into
n to testify against him, and then ride back home.
etimes you rode four or five hundred miles just to get
one criminal taken care of.

It was thought much easier to hang the man when and
re he was caught, and that was often done. It saved
r horse and saved your time.

They were hanging Leo Carver
Tuesday afternoon, and the loafers were watching the
lows go up. This was the first official hanging in the
tory of Canyon Gap, and the first gallows ever built in
e Territory. But then, the citizens at the Gap were
vays the kind to go in for style.

The boys from the ranches were coming in, and the
·d-booted men from the mines, and the nine saloons
re closing up, but only for the hour of the hanging. On
e street behind the Palace where the cottonwoods lined
e creek, Fat Marie had given three hours off to the girls.
e for the hanging and one for mourning and the third
drinking their tears away.

For Leo had been a spending man who would be
ssed along the street, and Leo had been a singing man
h a voice as clear as a mountain echo and fresh as
ong wind through the sage. And Leo was a handsome
n, with a gun too quick to his hand. So they were
aging Leo Carver on the gallows in Canyon Gap, and
folks were coming in from the forks of every creek.

From behind the barred window Leo watched them
rking. "Build it high!" he yelled at them. "And build it
ong, for you're hanging the best man in Canyon Gap
en tomorrow comes!"

Old Pap, who had prospected in the Broken Hills
ore the first foundation was laid at the Gap, took his
e from his mouth and spat into the dust. "He's right, at
t," he said, "and no lie. If the 'Paches were coming

193

over that hill right now, it's Leo Carver I'd rather ha
beside me than any man jack in this town."

Editor Chafee nodded his head. "Nobody will de
that he's a fighting man," he agreed. "Leo was all rig
until civilization caught up with him."

And there it was said, a fit epitaph for him, if epita
he'd have, and in their hearts not a man who heard it b
agreed that what Chafee said was right.

"There'll be some," Old Pap added, "who'll feel a si
of relief when they spring that trap. When Leo's neck
stretched and the sawbones says the dead word over hi
many a man will stop sweating, you can bet on that."

"Better be careful what you say." Jase Ford shift
uneasily. "It ain't healthy to be hintin'."

"Not since they put Leo away, it ain't," Old P
agreed, "but truth's a luxury the old can afford. Ther
nothing they can take from me but my life, and tha
no use to me. And to do that they'd have to sh
me down from behind, and that's the sort of thing the
do unless they could hang me legal, like Leo Carver's
be hung."

Nobody said anything, but Chafee looked gloomy as
stared at the gallows. There was no living doubt that L
Carver was an outlaw. No doubt that he had rustled a f
head here and there, no doubt that he had offended t
nice people of the town by carousing at the Palace a
down the street of the cottonwoods. There was no dou
either, that he'd stuck up the stage that night on Rous
sock—but from there on there was doubt a-plenty.

Mitch Williams was dead, buried out there on boot
with the others gone before him—Mitch Williams,
shotgun messenger who never lost a payload until t
night on Rousensock, the night that Leo Carver stuck
the stage.

It was a strange story no matter how you looked at
but Leo was a strange man, a strange man of dark mo

d happy ones, but a man with a queer streak of gallantry
him and something of a manner all his own.

Mitch had been up on the box that night when Leo
rver stepped from the brush. Oh, he was wearing a
sk, all right, wearing a mask that covered his face. But
o did not know it was Leo?

He stepped from the brush with a brace of six-guns in
hands and said, "Hold those horses, Pete! You can—"
broke off sharp there, for he saw Mitch.

Now Mitch Williams was a hand. He had that shotgun
er his knees but the muzzle was away from Leo. Mitch
ıld never have swung that shotgun around under Leo's
n, and he knew it. So did Doc Spender, who was stage
ver. Leo Carver had that stage dead to rights and he
d Mitch Williams helpless.

"Sorry, Mitch!" He said it loud and clear, so they all
ard him. "I thought this was your night off. I'd never
a stage you were on, and I'd never shoot you or force
u to shoot me." He swung his horse. "So long!" And he
s gone.

That was Leo for you. That was why they liked him along
Gila, and why as far away as the Nueces they told
ries about him. But what happened after that was different.

The stage went on south. It went over the range through
-Shooter Gap and there was another holdup. There was
udden blast of fire from the rocks and Mitch Williams
pled dead from the box, and then another blast—it was
shotgun—and Doc took a header into the brush and
ıghed out his life there in the mesquite.

Inside they were sitting still and frightened. They heard
nebody crawl up to the box and throw it down. They
ard it hit, and then they heard somebody riding off.
e horse, one rider.

The next morning they arrested Leo.

He was washing up at the time, and they'd waited for
t that. He had his guns off and they took him without a
ht. Not that he tried to make one. He didn't. He just
ked surprised.

"Aw, fellers," he protested. "I never done nothin
What's the matter?"

"You call that nothing? You robbed the stage last night

"Oh, that?" He just grinned. "Put down those gun
boys. I'll come along. Sure, you know by this time I didr
rob it. I just stuck it up for a lark, and when I seen Mitc
I knowed it was no lark. That hombre would have sat st
while I robbed it and drilled me when I left. He was
trusty man, that one."

"You said 'was,' so I guess you know you killed him.

Leo's face changed then. "Killed who? Say, what
this?"

And then they told him, and his face turned gray a
sick. He looked around at their faces and none of the
were friendly. Mitch had been a family man, and so ha
Doc. Both of them well liked.

"I didn't do it," Leo said. "That was somebody else.
left 'em be."

"Until you could get a shotgun!" That was Mort Lewan
who shipped the money for the bank. "Like you sai
Mitch would shoot. You knew that, and he had the gun
you, so you backed out. Then you came back later with
shotgun and shot him from ambush."

"That's not true." Leo was dead serious. "And l
didn't have me covered. Mitch had that shotgun pointe
the other way. I had the drop and if I'd been planning
kill him, I'd've shot him then."

Oh, they had a trial! Judge come over from Tucson
hold court. They had a trial and a big one. Folks con
from all over, and they made a big thing of it. Not th
there was much anybody could say for Leo.

Funny thing, that is. Most of us, right down inside, v
knowed the kind of man Leo Carver was, but most of wh
we knew wasn't evidence. Ever stop to think how hard
is to know a man isn't a murderer and yet know that yo
feeling he isn't ain't evidence?

They made it sound bad. Leo admitted he had killed
ven men. Fair, stand-up fights, but still the men were
ead by his gun. He admitted to rustling a few cows. Leo
uld have denied it, and maybe they couldn't have proved
in a court of law, but Leo wasn't used to the ways of
urts and he knowed darn well we all knew he had
stled them cows. Fact is, I don't think he ever thought
denying it.

He had stuck up a few stages, too. He even admitted
that. But he denied killing Mitch Williams and he
nied getting that box.

Twenty thousand, it held. Twenty thousand in gold.

Everybody thought Webb Pascal would defend Leo,
t he refused, said he wanted no part of it. Webb had
ayed poker with Leo and they'd been friends, but Webb
fused him. Leo took that mighty hard. Lane Moore
fused him, too, so all he could do was get that drunken
d Bob Keyes to handle his case.

Convicted? You know he was. That's why they are
nging him. Keyes couldn't defend a sick cat from a bath.
hen they got through asking questions of Leo Carver,
 was a dead Injun, believe me.

He had tried to stick up the stage once. He was a
own killer. He had rustled cows. He traveled with a bad
ement in Canyon Gap. He had no alibi. All he had,
ally, was his own statement that he hadn't done it—that
d the thing we knew in our hearts that isn't admissible
evidence.

"Shame for you fellers to go to all that trouble," Leo
d now. That was Leo. There's no stopping him. "Why
n't we just call the whole thing off?"

Mort Lewand stood in his doorway chewing his cigar
d watching that gallows go up, and it made me sore,
eing it like that, for if ever one man had hated another,
ort Lewand had hated Leo.

Why? No particular reason. Personality, I'd guess you'd
. It was simply that they never tied up right. Mort, he
ched every dime he made. Leo spent his or gave it

away. Mort went to church regular and was a rising youn
businessman. He was the town's banker and he owned th
express company, and he had just bought one of the fine
ranches in the country.

Leo never kept any money. He was a cattleman whe
he wanted to be, and as steady a hand as you'd find whe
he worked. One time he saved the CY herd almost singl
handed when they got caught in a norther. He took on th
job of ramrodding the Widow Ferguson's ranch after he
old man was killed, and he tinkered and slaved and worke
doing the job of a half-dozen hands until she had some
thing she could see for money enough to keep her.

Leo never kept a dime. He ate it up, drank it up, gav
it away. The rest of the time he sat under the cottonwoo
and played that old guitar of his and sang songs, old song
like my mother used to sing, old Scotch, Irish, and En
glish songs, and some he made up as he went along.

He got into fights too. He whipped the three Tayl
boys singlehanded one day. I remember that most particu
lar because I was there. That was the day he got the bloc
on Ruth Hadlin's handkerchief.

The Hadlins were the town's society. Every town's g
some society, and Judge Emory Hadlin was the big man
this town. He had money, all right, but he had name to
Even in the West some folks set store by a name, an
whenever the judge said his name it was like ringing a b
gong. It had a sound. Maybe that was all some names ha
but this one had more.

Honor, reputation, square dealing, and no breath
scandal ever to touch any of them. Fine folks, and ever
body knew it. Mort Lewand, he set his cap for Ruth b
she never seemed to see him. That made him some a
gered, but tickled most of us. Mort figured he was migh
high-toned and it pleased us when Ruth turned him dov
flat.

Don't get the idea she was uppity. There was that tin

l Pap come down with pneumonia. He was in a bad
y and nobody to look after him but little Mary Ryan
m down on the Street. Mary cared for him night and
almost until Ruth Hadlin heard about it.

She came down there and knocked on the door, and
en Mary opened it and saw Ruth she turned seven
ors. There she was, a mighty pert little girl, but she
s from the Street, and here was Ruth Hadlin—well,
y don't come any further apart.

Mary flushed and stammered and she didn't know
at to say, but Ruth came right on in. She turned around
said, "How is he, Mary? I didn't even know he was

Ill, that's what she said. We folks mostly said sick
tead of ill. Mary was shocked, too, never guessing that
body like Ruth would know her name, or speak to her
that.

"He's bad off, Miss Ruth, but you shouldn't be here.
s is the—it's the Street."

Ruth just looked at her and smiled, and she said, "I
w it is, Mary, but Old Pap is ill and he can be just as ill
the Street as anywhere. I just heard about it, Mary,
how you've been caring for him. Now you go get some
. I'll stay with him."

Mary hesitated, looking at that beautiful blue gown
h was wearing and at the shabby little cabin. "There
t—isn't much to do," she protested.

"I know." Ruth was already bending over Old Pap
she just looked around and said, "By the way,
ry, tell somebody to go tell Doctor Luther to come
n here."

"We tried, miss. He won't come. He said all his busi-
s was the other side of town, that he'd no time for
n here."

Ruth straightened up then. "You go tell him that Ruth
llin wants him down here!" Her voice was crisp. "He'll
e."

He did, too.

But that was Miss Ruth. She was a thoroughbred, th
one. And that was where she first met Leo Carver.

It was the third day she had been sharing the nursi
with Mary Ryan, and she was in the shack alone when s
heard that horse. He was coming hell bent for electi
and she heard him pull up in front of the house and th
the door opened and in stepped Leo Carver.

She knew him right off. How could you miss him? I
was two inches over six feet, with shoulders wider th
two of most men, and he was dark and clean-built wit
fine line to his jaw and he had cold gray eyes. He w
two guns and his range clothes, and right then he ha
two-day growth of beard. It must have startled her. H
was a man known as an outlaw, a rustler, and a killer, a
she was there alone with a sick man.

He burst in that door and then drew up short, look
from Ruth to the sick old man. If he was surprised to fi
her there, he didn't let on. He just swept off his hat a
asked, "How is he, Miss Hadlin?"

For some reason she was excited. Frightened, may
"He's better," she said. "Miss Ryan and I have be
nursing him."

Mary had come into the room behind him, and n
she stepped around quickly. "He's a lot better, Leo," :
said.

"Maybe I can help nurse him, then," Carver sa
He was looking at Ruth and she was white-faced and lar
eyed.

Old Pap opened one eye. "Like hell," he said expr
sively. "You think I want a relapse? You get on out
here. Seems like," he protested plaintively, "every tim
git to talk to a good-lookin' gal, somebody comes hor
in!"

Leo grinned then and looked from Ruth to Ma
"He's in his right mind, anyway," he said, and left.

Mary stood there looking at Ruth, and Ruth loo
after Leo and then at Mary.

"He's—he's an outlaw," Ruth said.

Mary Ryan turned very sharp toward Ruth, and I
kon it was the only time she ever spoke up to Ruth.
's the finest man I ever knew!"

And the two of them just stood there looking at each
er and then they went to fussing over Old Pap. That
the longest convalescence on record.

But there was that matter of the blood on her handker-
f. Ruth Hadlin was coming down the street and she
wearing a beautiful gray dress and a hat with a veil—
uptown and big city.

She was coming down the boardwalk and everybody
turning to look—she was a fine figure of a woman and
carried herself well—and just then the doors of the
ce burst open and out comes a brawling mass of men
ging with all their fists. They spilled past Ruth Hadlin
the street and it turns out to be the three Taylors and
Carver.

They hit dirt and came up swinging. Leo smashed a
fist into the face of Scott Taylor and he went over into
street. Bob rushed him and Leo ducked and took him
nd the knees, dumping him so hard the ground shook.

Bully Taylor was the tough one, and he and Leo stood
e a full half-minute slugging it out with both hands,
then Leo stepped inside and whipped one to Bully's
a and the pride of the Taylors hit dirt, out so cold he's
ably sleeping yet.

Ruth Hadlin had stopped in her tracks, and now Leo
ped back and wiped the blood from his face with a
and some of it spattered on Ruth's handkerchief. She
d out. He turned around and then he turned colors.

'Miss Hadlin," he said with a grin on his face, "I'm
t sorry. I'd no intention getting blood on you, but"
d he grinned—"it's good red blood, even if it isn't
."

She looked at him without turning a hair, and then she
coolly, "Don't stand there with your face all bloody.
wash it." And then she added just as coolly, "And next
don't lead with your right. If he hadn't been so all in,

he'd have knocked you out." With that she walks off
the street and we all stood there staring.

Leo, he stared most of all. "Well, I'm a skinned skun
he said. "Where do you reckon she ever heard ab
leading with a right?"

Mary Ryan, she heard about it, but she said nothi
just nothing at all, and that wasn't Mary's way. Of cou
we all knew about Mary. She was plumb crazy about I
but he paid no particular attention to any one of the gi
Or all of them, for that matter.

There was talk around town, but there always is. So
folks said this was as good a time as any to get shut of I
Carver and his like. That it was time Canyon Gap chan
its ways and spruced up a bit. Mort Lewand was alw
for changing things. He even wanted to change the na
of Canyon Gap to Hadlin. It was the judge himself v
stopped that.

So we sat around now and listened to the hammers
thought of how big an occasion it was to be. Some of
folks from the creek were already in town, camped
ready for the big doings tomorrow.

Ruth Hadlin was not around and none of us gav
much thought. All of this was so far away from the Ha
folks. Ruth bought a horse, I remember, about that ti
It was a fine big black. The Breed done sold it to her.

Funny thing, come to think of it, because I'd he
him turn down five hundred for that horse—and that
country where you get a good horse for twenty dolla
but Ruth had ways and nobody refused her very mu
What she wanted with a horse that big I never could s

Editor Chafee, he hoisted his britches and was star
back toward the shop when Ruth Hadlin came down
street. She stopped nearby and she looked at that gallo
Maybe her face was a little pale, but the fact that all th
roughnecks were around never seemed to bother her.

"Tom," she said right off, "what do you believe

·ver did with that money?" Chafee rubbed his jaw.
·u know," he scowled, "I've studied about that. I can't
itly say."

"What has he always done with it before?"

"Why, he spent it. Just as fast as he could."

"I wonder why he didn't use it to hire a better lawyer?
could have had a man from El Paso for that. Or for
ch less! A good lawyer might have freed him."

"I wondered about that." Chafee looked a little anx-
sly at Mort Lewand. Mort was a power in town and he
iked Carver and made no secret of it. Lewand was
king that way, and now he started over. "It doesn't
lly matter now, does it?" Chafee added.

Lewand came up and looked from one to the other.
·n he smiled at Ruth. "Rather noisy, isn't it, Ruth?
uld you like me to escort you home?"

"Why, thank you," she said sweetly, "but I think I'll
·. I've never seen a gallows before. Have you, Mr.
vand?"

"Me?" He looked startled. "Oh, yes. In several places."

She stood there a few minutes watching the carpenters
·k. "Well," Ruth said slowly, "it's too bad, but I'm glad
local people lost anything in that holdup."

We all looked at her, but she was watching the gal-
s, an innocent smile on her lips.

Editor Chafee cleared his throat. "I guess you weren't
, Miss Hadlin. The fact is, that money belonged to
·t here."

She smiled brightly. Women are strange folk. "Oh, no,
1. You've been misinformed! As a matter of fact, that
1ey was a payment on Mr. Lewand's ranch, and when
:onsigned it for carriage it became the property of the
1er owner of the ranch. That was the agreement, wasn't
/Ir. Lewand?"

For some reason it made Mort mad, but he nodded.
at's right."

Ruth nodded too. "Yes, Mr. Lewand was telling me
ut it. He's very farsighted, I think. Isn't that wonder-

ful, Tom? Just think how awful it would have been if
had paid that whole twenty thousand dollars and then l
it and had to pay it over! My, it would take a wealthy m
to do that, wouldn't it now?"

Editor Chafee was looking thoughtful all of a sudde
and Old Pap had taken the pipe from his lips and v
staring at Ruth. Mort, he looked mad as a horny to
though for the life of me, I couldn't see why. After all
had been a smart stunt.

"Those awful shotguns!" From the way she was talk
you wouldn't have believed that girl had a brain in I
head. "I don't believe people should be allowed to o
them. I wonder where Leo got the one he used?"

"Claimed he never owned one," Chafee commen
slowly.

"He probably borrowed one from a friend," Mort s
carelessly. "I suppose they are easy to find."

"That's just it!" Ruth exclaimed. "The man who loar
him that shotgun is just as guilty as he is. I think sor
thing should be done about it."

"I doubt if anybody loaned him one," Mort said,
hand. "He probably stole it."

"Oh, no! Because," she added hastily, "if he did,
returned it. Everybody in town who owns a shotgun :
has it. There are only six of them in Canyon Gap. Dac
has two, Editor Chafee has one, Pap here has an
broken one, and Mitch always carried one."

"That's only five," Old Pap said softly.

"Oh!" Ruth put her fingers to her mouth. "How silly
me. I'd forgotten yours, Mr. Lewand."

There was the stillest silence I ever did hear, w
nobody looking at anybody else. Suddenly Ruth lookec
a little watch she had, gasped something about being la
and started off.

Editor Chafee began to fill his pipe, and Old l
scratched his knee, and all of us just sat there looking a
dumber than we were. Mort Lewand didn't seem to kn
what to say, and what he finally said didn't help much.

ıan wanted to find a shotgun," he said, "I don't suppose
d have much trouble." With that he turned and walked

You know something? The sound of those hammers
sn't a good sound. Editor Tom Chafee scratched his
n with the stem of his pipe. "Pete," he says to me, "you
re supposed to ride shotgun that night. Whose shotgun
uld you have used?"

"Mitch always lent me his. I was feeling poorly and
tch took over for me. Leo, he called my name when he
t rode up, if you recall."

That shotgun business was bothering all of us. Where
' Leo get a shotgun? This was rifle and pistol country,
l shotguns just weren't plentiful. Ruth Hadlin could
'e narrowed it down even more, because everybody
w that Judge Hadlin wouldn't let anybody touch one of
guns but himself. They were expensive, engraved guns,
l he kept them locked up in a case.

Where had Leo picked up a shotgun? What had he
ie with the money?

Editor Chafee looked down at Old Pap all of a sudden.
p," he said, "let's walk over to my place. You, too,
e. I want you to look at my shotgun."

We looked at that gun and she was all covered with
ase and dust. That shotgun hadn't been fired in six
ıths, anyway. Or for a long time. It certainly hadn't
·n the gun that killed Mitch and Doc.

"Just for luck," Chafee said seriously, "we'd better go
e a look at the judge's guns."

Behind us we could hear those hammers a-pounding,
we could hear O'Brien rehearsing his German band.
m where we walked we could see six or seven wagons
ıing down the road, all headed into Canyon Gap, for
hanging.

Certain things happened that I didn't hear until later. I
ı't hear about Ruth Hadlin, all pretty as ever a picture

could be, walking into that jail to see Leo Carver. Wh
she got into the office the sheriff was standing there loo
ing down at a cake on his desk. That cake had been
and it was some broken up because he had taken two fi
from it. Mary Ryan was standing by his side.

Sheriff Jones looked mighty serious. "Mary," he w
saying, "this here's a criminal offense, helping a man
break jail. Now, where's those other two files? No use y
stalling—I know you bought four of 'em."

"You're so smart," she said, "you find 'em!" She toss
her head at him and gave him a flash of those saucy eyes
hers.

Sheriff Jones leaned over the table. "Now look, Mar
he protested, "I don't want to make trouble for you, l
we just can't have no prison break. Why, think of all th
folks coming for miles to see a hanging! They'd be m
enough to string *me* up."

"Why not?" she said, short-like. "He's no more gu
than you are."

Jones started to protest again and then he looked
and saw Ruth Hadlin standing there in the door. Her fa
was cool as she could make it, and, mister, that was co
In one hand she held Leo's guitar.

The sheriff straightened up, mighty flustered. Here
was, talking confidential-like with a girl from the Stre
Suppose that got around among the good folks of t
town. Be as much as his job was worth, and electi
coming up too.

He flushed and stammered. "This here—this you
woman," he spluttered, "she was trying to smuggle files
the prisoner. She—"

Ruth Hadlin interrupted, her eyes cold and queenl
on the sheriff. "I can assure you, Sheriff Jones, that I
not at all interested in your relations with this young la
nor in the subject of your conversation.

"I have brought this guitar to the prisoner," she co
tinued. "I understand he enjoys singing, and we think
cruel and inhuman that he be forced to listen to th

ging and hammering while they build a gallows on
ch to hang him. It is cruel torture."

Jones was embarrassed. "He don't mind, ma'am," he
tested. "Leo, he's—"

"May I take this instrument to him, Sheriff Jones?"
voice was cold. "Or do you want to examine me? Do
think I might be smuggling files too?"

Sheriff Jones was embarrassed. The very idea of laying
and on Ruth Hadlin, the daughter of old Judge Emory
llin, gave him cold shivers.

"No, no, ma'am! Of course not." He gestured toward
cells. "Just you give it to him, ma'am! I'm sorry. I—"

"Thank you, Sheriff." Ruth swept by him and up to the

"Young man,"—her voice was clear—"I understand
you play a guitar, so I have brought you this one. I
e the music that you get out of it will make your heart
"

Leo looked startled, and he took the guitar through the
. "Thank you, Miss Hadlin," he said politely. "I wish—"
broke off, his face a little flushed. "I wish you didn't
e to see me in here. You see, I didn't—I never killed
e men. I'd like you to believe that."

"What I believe," Ruth said sweetly, "is of no impor-
e. The music from the guitar will be pleasant for you,
ayed in private." She turned abruptly and walked out,
she went by Sheriff Jones like a pay-car past a tramp.

Mary told it afterwards, and Mary said that Leo plunked
ring on that guitar and then he looked at it, funny-
"It sure didn't sound right," Mary said. I shouldn't
der.

That was late Monday afternoon. By sundown there
maybe two hundred people camped around town
ing for the big hanging next afternoon. Old Pap, he
n't around, nor was Editor Chafee. Some said that
n they left the judge's house, the judge himself was
ig with them.

When next I come across Old Pap, he was standing on

the corner looking at that gallows. That was near the j
and from the window Leo could see us.

"Folks would be mighty upset if they missed tl
hanging, Pap," Leo said.

"They won't!" Pap was mighty short and gruff. "The
git their hanging, and don't you forget it."

That gallows looked mighty ghostly standing there
the twilight, and it didn't make me feel no better. L
well, he always seemed a right nice feller. Of course,
had rustled a few head, but I wouldn't want to take
oath I hadn't, nor Old Pap, nor most of us. Leo, he
just a young hellion, that was all.

Even when he stuck up those stages he just done it
drinking money. Not that I'm saying it's right, becaus
know it ain't, but them days and times, folks excused a
of a young man who was full of ginger, long as he di
hurt nobody and was man enough.

Especially of Leo's sort. If you was in trouble you
let him know. Come prairie fire, flood, stampede,
whatever, Leo was your man. No hour was too late, no
too miserable for him to lend a hand. And never tal
dime for it.

So we all went to bed, and the last thing Leo said v
"I never did cotton to no rope necktie. I don't figure
becoming."

"Wait'll tomorry," Old Pap said.

The sun was no more than up before the lid blew
the town. Somebody yelled and folks came a-runnin
slid into my pants and scrambled outside. The crowd
streaming toward the Plaza and I run down there v
'em. The bars was out of the jail window, filed off clea
you'd wish, then bent back out of the way. Tied to on
them was a sheet of paper. It was a note:

"Sorry I couldn't wait, but I don't think you folks v
me hanging around here, anyway."

Mary Ryan was there by the jail. She had tears in

but she looked pleased as a polecat in a henhouse
Sheriff Jones, he took on something fierce.

'Figured she was talking poetry," he said angrily. "She
him the music he'd get out of that guitar would make
heart free. No wonder Mary wouldn't tell me what
ame of the other two files."

One big bearded man with hard eyes stared at the
iff with a speculative eye. "What about the hanging?"
demanded. "We drove fifty mile to see a hanging."

Editor Tom Chafee, Judge Emory Hadlin, and Old
came up around them. They looked across the little
e at Jones.

"Ruth figured it right," the judge said. "Only six shot-
s in town. My two shotguns, and by the dust of the
s you can see they'd not been disturbed; Editor
fee's, which hadn't been cleaned in months; Old Pap's
broke, and Mitch had his with him. That leaves just
more shotgun."

Everybody just stood there, taking it all in and doing
e figuring. Suppose that twenty thousand never left
bank? Or suppose it did leave and it was recovered by
man sending it? His debt would be paid and he would
have the money, and a young scamp like Leo Carver'd
blamed for it all.

Of course, Leo was gone. Some folks said he rode that
black Ruth Hadlin bought. What happened to that
e we never did know, because Ruth was gone, too,
her gray mare.

The trail headed west, the trail they left, and some-
y living on the edge of town swore he heard two voices
ing something about being bound for Californy.

We figured the judge would about burst a gasket, but
as a most surprising man. Something was said about it
omebody and all he did was smile a little.

Many's a thoroughbred," he said, "was a frisky colt.
e they get the bridle on 'em, they straighten out. As
s that goes," he added, "every blue-blooded family
use a little red blood!"

So everybody was happy. We celebrated mighty bi
reckon the biggest in the history of Canyon Gap. O'Bri
German band played, and everybody had plenty to
and drink.

The folks that came for the hanging wasn't disappoin
either. They got what they wanted. They got their ha
ing, all right. Maybe it wasn't a legal hanging, but it
sure satisfactory.

We hung Mort Lewand.

About Louis L'Amour

...nk of myself in the oral tradition—as a troubadour, a village taleteller, ...an in the shadows of the campfire. That's the way I'd like to be ...nbered—as a storyteller. A good storyteller."

...s doubtful that any author could be as at home in the world recreated in ...ovels as Louis Dearborn L'Amour. Not only could he physically fill the ...of the rugged characters he wrote about, but he literally "walked the ...ny characters walk." His personal experiences as well as his lifelong ...ion to historical research combined to give Mr. L'Amour the unique ...ledge and understanding of people, events, and the challenge of the ...ican frontier that became the hallmarks of his popularity.

...French-Irish descent, Mr. L'Amour could trace his own family in ...America back to the early 1600s and follow their steady progression ...vard, "always on the frontier." As a boy growing up in Jamestown, ...Dakota, he absorbed all he could about his family's frontier heritage, ...ling the story of his great-grandfather who was scalped by Sioux ...rs.

...rred by an eager curiosity and desire to broaden his horizons, Mr. ...ur left home at the age of fifteen and enjoyed a wide variety of jobs ...ing seaman, lumberjack, elephant handler, skinner of dead cattle, ...ment miner, and officer on tank destroyers during World War II. ...g his "yondering" days he also circled the world on a freighter, sailed a ...on the Red Sea, was shipwrecked in the West Indies and stranded in ...lojave Desert. He won fifty-one of fifty-nine fights as a professional ...and worked as a journalist and lecturer. He was a voracious reader and ...tor of rare books. His personal library contained 17,000 volumes.

...L'Amour "wanted to write almost from the time I could talk." After ...oping a widespread following for his many frontier and adventure ...s written for fiction magazines, Mr. L'Amour published his first full-...novel, *Hondo,* in the United States in 1953. Every one of his more ...00 books is in print; there are nearly 230 million copies of his books in ...worldwide, making him one of the bestselling authors in modern ...y history. His books have been translated into twenty languages, and ...than forty-five of his novels and stories have been made into feature ...and television movies.

...hardcover bestsellers include *The Lonesome Gods, The Walking ...* (his twelfth-century historical novel) *Jubal Sackett, Last of the Breed,* ...e Haunted Mesa. His memoir, *Education of a Wandering Man,* was a ...g bestseller in 1989. Audio dramatizations and adaptations of many ...ur stories are available on cassette tapes from Bantam Audio ...hing.

...recipient of many great honors and awards, in 1983 Mr. L'Amour ...e the first novelist ever to be awarded the Congressional Gold Medal ...United States Congress in honor of his life's work. In 1984 he was also ...ed the Medal of Freedom by President Reagan.

...is L'Amour died on June 10, 1988. His wife, Kathy, and their two ...en, Beau and Angelique, carry the L'Amour tradition forward with ...ooks written by the author during his lifetime to be published by ...m well into the nineties—among them, three additional Hopalong ...ly novels: *The Trail to Seven Pines, The Riders of High Ridge,* and ...e Shooter.

A Preview of
a Full-Length Louis L'Amour Western
A Brand-New Bantam Hardcover

THE RUSTLERS
OF WEST FORK

A Hopalong Cassidy Novel

On Sale Wednesday, May 22, 1991

Long out of print and now published for the first time under the author's own name, here is THE RUSTLERS OF WEST FORK, a Hopalong Cassidy novel written by Louis L'Amour. This classic frontier novel is as authentically detailed as it is action-packed, and features one of the most fondly remembered fictional cowboys.

In this first of four L'Amour Hopalong Cassidy novels, the cowpuncher heads west to deliver a fortune in bank notes to his old friend Dick Jordan. He soon learns that Jordan and his daughter Pam are being held prisoners on their Circle J ranch by a desperate band of outlaws.

The original creation of Clarence E. Mulford, Hopalong Cassidy became a national institution through movies and a weekly television series based on the many novels Mulford wrote. Mulford chose the young Louis L'Amour to continue Hopalong's adventures in print after he decided to retire.

Here, now, is THE RUSTLERS OF WEST FORK . . .

Hopalong Cassidy watched the old banker count the money with careful fingers. Fifteen thousand dollars was an amount to be handled with reverence and respect, and as he watched the mounting stack of bills, Hopalong saw them less as the long green bills they were than as the cattle they represented—the cattle and the work. Into that stack of bills was going money that had grown from days of cold wind and rain, nights of thunder and lightning, of restless herds poised for stampede, of rivers and washes running brim full with roaring flood waters, of dust, glistering sun, and the roar of rustlers' guns.

Into that pile so flat and green went more than money. Into that pile went months of brutal labor, the brindle steer that had killed a horse under him down in Lonetree Canyon, and the old mossyhorn who had fouled Lanky's rope on a juniper, putting him three weeks in bed with a broken leg. And into that pile went the kid from Toyah, who had ridden up to join them so full of vitality and exuberance, only to have his horse step into a prairie-dog hole while running ahead of a stampede. They had buried what was left of the kid and sent his hat and gun to a brother in El Paso.

"There she is, Hoppy," the banker said at last. "Buck will be mighty glad to get shut of that debt, I know. He's a man who takes bein' in debt harder'n any man I can think of, an' he's sure scrimped an' cut corners to have that much in three years!"

"Yeah," Cassidy agreed. "Buck's right conscientious about most things. He don't like to get into debt in the first place, but you know how it was with Dick Jordan. When he fell heir to that ranch out West he just up an' took off. He sold his cattle an' remuda to Buck, knowin' if there was one man around he could trust to pay ever' last red cent it was Buck.

"Came at a good time too. Buck had been talkin' about more cattle, an' with the additional range he could use, it would be a positive shame not to have 'em. Otherwise, he never would have gone into debt."

"You takin' this money West yourself?" The banker's shrewd old eyes studied the silver head. "I know Buck can't afford to be away right now."

"Yeah, I'm takin' it West, an' glad of the chance. Old Dick was a friend of mine, too, an' I've heard a sight about that ranch o' his. Rightly, it belonged to his wife, It was part of an old Spanish grant, you know."

"Uh-huh. Helped draw up some o' the papers. Got a daughter now, I hear."

"Had her a long time. Shucks, she was fourteen or fifteen before they left here."

"Say"—the banker turned around in his chair—"who's goin' out there with you?"

"With me? I'm goin' alone. Mesquite's off somewheres, as usual, an' Buck can't spare two men. Anyway, it ain't a two-man job."

"Maybe. Things out thataway are pretty lively. Had a letter from a friend of mine out to McClellan. Had his bank held up about three weeks ago, killed his cashier, wounded a deputy sheriff, then lost the durned posse."

"Lost 'em?"

"Uh-huh, just plain lost 'em."

Hopalong slid off the desk and gathered up the money. "Well, Buck will be waitin' for me, so I'd better get into the leather an' ride to the ranch. But don't you worry about this money. I'll see it gets to Dick, as promised."

Tucking the packages of bills into his black shirt and drawing his belt tighter, he hitched his guns into an easier position on his dark-trousered hips and started for the door.

The banker arose from his chair and walked to the window where he could watch Cassidy cross the street. The same trim bowed legs, the broad, sloping shoulders, the lean waist and choppy walk of the horseman. His silver guns were worn by much handling, and his boots were cracked and dusty. Suddenly the banker found himself wishing he was younger and starting west with Hopalong on that ride.

As he started to turn from the window a movement caught his eye, and he hesitated. A man had stepped out from beside the bank and started slowly across the street in Hopalong's wake. If that man had been standing alongside the bank, he might have seen Hopalong take the money, for there was an office window near the desk. The banker frowned. His wife would be waiting supper, and if he got into the saloon he might not get out for hours. . . . Anyway, Hopalong could take care of himself. He always had.

Trouble followed Hopalong Cassidy like wolves follow a snow-driven herd, but few men were more fitted to cope with it than the silver-haired gunfighter. He should have told Hoppy to look up Monaghan, at the bank in McClellan. Well, he could write to him. Maybe Hoppy would have business over that way.

Dusk was softening the line of the buildings when Hopalong crossed the street to the saloon. A poker game was in session when he pushed through the batwing doors, but the players carefully avoided his eyes. They knew each other, and knew the game was fairly even all around. But Hopalong was a specialist at draw. His brand of poker was apt to be expensive for them, and they wanted none of that.

Three men lounged at the bar, all strangers. One

of them, Hoppy remembered, had passed him on the step. His casual glance read their brands with a quick, easy eye, and he grinned to himself. Drifting punchers, maybe a shade on the owl-hoot side.

Trail dust lay thick on their clothes, but their guns had been wiped clean, and the cartridges in their belts shone brightly. One man—who had passed him on the walk before the saloon—was a slender young fellow with straight, clean-cut features and a deep line at one corner of his mouth. When he glanced toward Cassidy, Hopalong saw that one eye was half closed by a lowered lid. A first the man seemed to be winking. and then Hoppy realized the affliction was permanent.

The other two also had the look of hard cases. The tall man was round-shouldered and his face carried deep-set lines of cruelty and harshness. The third stranger was scarcely more than a boy, but one already far gone down the hard trails by the look of him.

Drifters were not uncommon, and the range life was not one calculated to make men soft. Such men as these came in and drifted on each morning and night, for Twin Rivers was on a trail much traveled in these months.

"Pullin' out tomorrow, Hoppy?" The bartender leaned his arms on the bar. "Johnny was sayin' you were headed West to visit Dick Jordan."

At the name all three strangers turned sharply to stare at Hopalong. Their expressions excited his interest and also their apparent familiarity with the name of Dick Jordan. Only a familiar name could have turned them so sharply. They looked away, and the man with the squint eye spoke to the others in a low, careful voice, as though explaining something.

"Yeah." said Cassidy, "we bought his herd three years ago. Buck wants me to ride out there, and that country always did appeal to me. It will be good to get shut of this dust and fill my lungs with that good mountain air again."

"Dick bought hisself a good ranch, I hear."

"He didn't buy it. His wife was Spanish an' the ranch was part of an old land grant belonging to her family. She inherited it, so they just moved out there. They took their daughter with them. She was maybe fifteen years old. Nice kid, but all knees and freckles."

One of the strangers snickered, and Cassidy glanced at them appraisingly. Two of them avoided his eyes, but the one with the bad eyelid met his glance boldly. "Heerd what y' said about ridin' to see Dick Jordan," he commented dryly, "an' if I was you. I'd forget it. That there's a tough country for drifters. They don't cotton to 'em, not none a-tall!"

"That right?" Hopalong said carelessly. "Well maybe I can help them get used to it."

The tall man answered him, and his eyes were hard as he looked at Cassidy. "You go out there huntin' him," he said insolently, "an' you're sure likely to find him! You're liable to go right where he is!" As he finished speaking he put down his glass and all three walked out of the saloon. On the walk outside one of them spoke, and then all laughed.

Cassidy glanced at the bartender. "Know those fellers?"

"Been around all afternoon," the bartender explained, "an' takin' in a lot of room. The squinty one, he's gettin' his horse shod. Then they're driftin' on, headin' West."

Hopalong accepted the information and turned it over in his mind. Suppose they knew he had the money? They might be honest cowhands just feeling their oats in a strange town, but all Hopalong's instincts told him they were more than that, and men to be reckoned with. Nor was he the man to underrate anyone. Considering the problem, he decided that if they were planning to rob him they would do it tonight, and probably right now. There was nothing to be gained by keeping them waiting. With a plan of the town in his mind, he did a few minutes of rapid thinking, then turned and waved good night to the bartender and stepped outside.

Opposite the saloon a man sat beside a saddled horse. As Hopalong stepped out, the man drew deep on his cigarette, and it glowed with sudden, sharp brightness, Cassidy noticed it with a wry curling at the corners of his mouth. A signal. Who did they think he was? A pilgrim? A soft-tailed tenderfoot? He stepped down beside his horse and tightened the saddle girth, watching the man out of the corners of his eyes.

There were only three places men might wait where that cigarette signal could be seen. There was narrow opening beyond the hardware store down the street. Farther along the entrance to the alley by the livery stable was another, and up the street by the sheriff's office was the third. Nobody but a fool would wait by the livery stable, for the other end of that alley was closed off by the horse corrals. The night was cool, and that puncher across the street would have been there for only one reason, to warn the others that Cassidy had come out. Necessarily, they would have to be ready no matter which way he turned, so one man must be up the street, the other down.

The spot by the hardware store and the alley by the sheriff's office would be the places. One man to stop him and two to close in. He grinned at the simplicity of it. Would the fellow stick a gun into him? Or merely ask for a light to give others time to come up?

Hopalong tightened the cinch, and then, as he put a foot in the stirrup, he suddenly seemed to remember something. He took down his foot, stepped up on the boardwalk, and went back into the saloon. Scarcely aware of the surprised glances, he walked swiftly through the room to the back, and turning, as if to enter the office, he went past it into a narrow passage from which a door opened at the back.

Careful not to allow his spurs to jingle, he walked swiftly toward the sheriff's office. When behind it he looked up the narrow alleyway between the buildings and caught the dark outline of the man who was waiting there. A hard grin parted his lips, and he moved up behind the man. "Huntin' somebody?" he asked softly.

The squint-eyed man whirled swiftly, his hand

ropping for his gun, and Hopalong struck with a
ork-hardened fist. It caught the man flush on
he chin and his knees sagged, letting his jaw
own to meet the lifting right. As though his legs
ad turned to limp rubber. the man slumped to the
round, and Hopalong stepped swiftly past him to
he corner.

Across the street the cigarette smoker, having heard
ounds or the brief scuffle, was on his feet, starting
ward him. He stepped out past his horse. "Bizco?"
e called softly. "What's up?"

Hopalong stepped easily into the street. "I am,"
e said. "Did y' wish to see me?"

It was the youngster of the lot, and the least
perienced. Instead of brazening it out, he felt him-
lf trapped, and his own guilty reaction betrayed
m. His hand dropped for his gun.

The tall man down the street was already aware
at something had gone wrong, and had stepped
t from cover and started toward them. When he
w Hopalong Cassidy he knew that somehow their
an had miscarried, and like his younger friend, he
abbed for his six-shooter.

Neither man saw the blur of movement as Hopalong
assidy drew. His guns came up, spouting flame
en as theirs cleared leather, and his first shot was
 the tall man, who he rightly deduced was the
ore dangerous of the two. The shot struck just
ove the glisten of the belt buckle and the second
t the edge of the first. In almost the same instant
opalong's other gun had roared, and the younger

man went to his knees. He tried a shot that tugge
at Cassidy's sleeve. Then he spilled over in the dus
losing his grip on his pistol.

Wheeling, Hoppy jumped back into the alley . .

TO BE CONTINUED . . .
Beginning Wednesday, May 22, 1991
Wherever Bantam Hardcovers are sold.

Look for the Bantam Rooster
for the *Only* Authorized

LOUIS L'AMOUR

Short Story Collections Anywhere

Buy them at your local bookstore or use these pages for ordering:

antam Books, Dept. LL23, 414 East Golf Road, Des Plaines, IL 60016

lease send me the items I have checked above. I am enclosing $_____
lease add $2.50 to cover postage and handling). Send check or money
der, no cash or C.O.D.s please.

r/Ms _____

ddress _____

ty/State _____ Zip _____

                                                              LL23–6/91
ease allow four to six weeks for delivery.
ices and availability subject to change without notice.

LOUIS L'AMOUR

BANTAM'S #1
ALL-TIME BESTSELLING AUTHOR
AMERICA'S FAVORITE FRONTIER WRITER

☐	27518	THE LONESOME GODS	$4.95
☐	24133	LAW OF THE DESERT BORN	$3.50
☐	28031	TO TAME A LAND	$3.50
☐	23132	SHADOW RIDERS	$3.99
☐	27561	COMSTOCK LODE	$4.95
☐	28104	YONDERING	$3.50
☐	24763	MILO TALON	$3.50
☐	25200	THE STRONG SHALL LIVE	$3.50
☐	26446	BENDIGO SHAFTER	$4.99
☐	25098	THE KEY-LOCK MAN	$3.50
☐	28082	RADIGAN	$3.99
☐	25393	WAR PARTY	$3.50
☐	24905	KIOWA TRAIL	$3.99
☐	28210	THE BURNING HILLS	$3.50
☐	24858	SHALAKO	$3.50
☐	24867	KILRONE	$3.95
☐	25771	THE RIDER OF LOST CREEK	$3.50
☐	24759	CALLAGHEN	$3.50
☐	28084	THE QUICK AND THE DEAD	$3.50
☐	25321	OVER ON THE DRY SIDE	$3.99
☐	28081	DOWN THE LONG HILLS	$3.50
☐	24766	WESTWARD THE TIDE	$3.50
☐	24748	KID RODELO	$3.99
☐	24847	BROKEN GUN	$3.99
☐	28172	WHERE THE LONG GRASS BLOWS	$3.99
☐	26913	HOW THE WEST WAS WON	$4.50

Buy them at your local bookstore or use this page to order:

Bantam Books, Dept. LL2, 414 East Golf Road, Des Plaines, IL 60016

Please send me the items I have checked above. I am enclosing $_____
(please add $2.50 to cover postage and handling). Send check or money
order, no cash or C.O.D.s please.

Mr/Ms _____

Address _____

City/State_____ Zip _____

LL2-5/91

Please allow four to six weeks for delivery.
Prices and availability subject to change without notice.